Pelmanism

Pelmanism

DILYS ROSE

Luath Press Limited

EDINBURGH

www.luath.co.uk

All characters appearing in this work are fictitious.
Any resemblance to real persons, living or dead, is purely
coincidental.

First published 2014

ISBN: 978-1-910021-23-1

The publisher acknowledges the support of

ALBA | CHRUTHACHAIL

towards the publication of this book.

The paper used in this book is recyclable.
It is made from low chlorine pulps
produced in a low energy, low emission manner
from renewable forests.

Printed and bound by
CPI Antony Rowe, Chippenham

Typeset in 10.5 point Sabon

for my friends

Acknowledgements

Sincere thanks are due for various help and support, to the following people: Geraldine Cooke, Louise Hutcheson, Sara Maitland, Jenni Calder, Jennie Renton, Barbara Imrie, Joan, James and Dorothy Parr, and Sally Whitton.

I would also like to thank the administrators and caretakers of Ledig House and Le Château de Lavigny, for greatly appreciated writing space and time, and for great food, views and company.

Homage to R.D. Laing

whatever they do
they must not no matter what
let him know they think
something's not right

whatever they know
they must not no matter what
let him think they know
something's not right

whatever they think
they must not no matter what
let him know they know
something he doesn't

Dilys Rose

Oilseed Rape and Porridge Oats

GALA'S MOTHER IS waiting on the station platform, though the plan was to meet at the car park and avoid a grand public reunion. As Vera Price is the only person meeting the train it doesn't matter much, and she has waited a while for this moment. She waves frantically and Gala can't help slowing down, postponing the moment of contact. Her mother looks smaller than she remembers her. Thinner. Her hair has turned a gun-metal grey and she's had it cut, in an androgynous, institutional chop. In pressed ecru trousers and a short-sleeved aqua shirt, she could be anybody's mother but she is Gala's, waving and smiling widely and hurrying towards her daughter, who puts down her weekend bag to receive an awkward hug.

Let me look at you!

Vera takes a step back but keeps a firm hold on Gala's shoulders, as if her daughter might turn tail, bolt along the platform and leap onto the train which is huffing and puffing and preparing to pull away from the platform. The thought does cross Gala's mind. The longer she stays away, the harder it is to come home. No, not home; back. This place was never her home. In her absence, while she was gallivanting on another continent with no clear plans for the future, her parents moved house again, this time relocating to the other side of the country, to the quaint coastal town, where they met. On the beach.

Then, horses were involved. The other, less romantic reasons for the move, are rarely mentioned.

You've cut your hair!

Yes, says her mother. I don't like it but it's easier. Anyway, nobody cares what you look like at my age. You've lost weight! She tries to wrestle Gala's bag into her possession. How long are you staying?

Just a couple of days.

Couldn't you make it a bit longer?

Not this time. I've a lot to sort out –

It's been so long since we've seen you. And Dad –

Again she tries to take control of the luggage, to make it her responsibility, her burden.

I can manage, Mum. I've been carrying my own bag for long enough.

Only trying to help. Are you working?

Not yet. I'll get something soon.

There's a lot of unemployment now. Mrs Thatcher says –

I really don't care what Mrs Thatcher says.

Her mother's lip wobbles, eyes pool. Why didn't she bite her tongue? Why wind up her mother about fucking Thatcher?

Sorry. But politics – is there any point in talking about politics?

No. Politics don't matter. Nobody ever keeps their promises, politicians or otherwise.

Gala stifles a sigh. When they are midway across the railway bridge, two fighter jets burst into the sky and roar overhead, close enough to feel the knock of displaced air. Ever sensitive to noise, her mother clamps her hands over her ears.

Such a racket, says Vera. We thought about getting a house over this way but the noise from the air base put us off. And Dad said being reminded of the RAF every minute of the day would be adding insult to injury. During the war he wanted to be a pilot but the air force didn't take him.

I know, Mum.

It's always irked him.

I know.

The jets disappear over the brow of the hill, leaving dirty black trails against an otherwise clear sky.

As Vera descends the clanking bridge, she takes Gala's arm. There's a waver of uncertainty in her step.

A grand day, she pipes up, bright but brittle. The countryside is at its best.

It's lovely.

The shimmering air has a salty tang. Poppies nod by the roadside. Fields of blue-green cabbage and ripe wheat sweep down to the coast where a frill of breaking waves edges a vivid, turquoise sea. All pretty as a picture but for a large, acid yellow field, so intense in colour that it looks artificial.

Rape, says Vera. Horrible. Gives me headaches. A cash crop. It's subsidised by the government. An eyesore. And people say it causes allergies.

She rummages in her bag, plucks out sunglasses with sugar-pink frames, sticks them on her straight, classical nose and stops in front of a shiny blue car. Prussian blue, Gala's father would call it.

Did we have this car the last time you were home?

I'm not sure.

Gala has never paid much attention to her parents' cars. Every couple of years they trade in their two-year-old model for a new one. Something to do with depreciation. Her parents are organised about such things: value for money, maintenance, repairs. Whatever else might be falling apart, their material world is in good enough nick.

The car smells of synthetic upholstery, pine air freshener and stale tobacco. The seats are hot, itchy. Gala rolls down the window, lets in the sea air.

Okay if I smoke?

You didn't quit? You said in your last letter that you were thinking of quitting.

No, Mum, I didn't quit.

Go on, then. Your father is back on the pipe. They only let him smoke out of doors. The grounds are really very nice, and very well kept, not a weed in sight, I don't know how they manage to keep the dandelions at bay, but he kicks up a fuss about all the rules and regulations. Especially the smoking policy. You'll see a change in him.

How has he been?

Up and down.

When do you think...? Gala lights up, inhales.

What? When do I think what?

Nothing. Nothing. Those poppies are pretty.

Say what you were going to say.

I was just wondering how long he's likely to be – how long they're likely to keep him.

Depends. On a number of things.

Her mother grips the steering wheel and crawls along, anxiously eyeing the needle of the speedometer.

Got to watch my speed around here. Speedtraps everywhere!

Mum, nobody in their right mind is ever going to do *you* for speeding!

What d'you mean their *right mind?*

Nothing. Sorry.

Her mother is the slowest driver in the world, which is not to say she's the most careful.

They caught your father. He got a ticket.

I thought you said he lost his licence.

He did. The speeding ticket was just the beginning. Did I tell you he turned the car over?

Maybe. I'm not sure I got all your letters. I was moving around a lot and the *poste restante* wasn't always reliable.

It was a write-off. He's lucky to be alive.

And no injuries?

Nothing to speak of.

He *was* lucky then, said Gala. Very lucky.

If you ask me the police did him a favour taking away his licence. At least until he sees reason. Whenever that's likely to be.

A whiff of something rank comes in the open window.

The paper mill's stinking today, says her mother, but it does produce lovely paper. Did you bring your sketchbooks? I'm sure Dad would love to see some sketches from your trip.

I don't have any. Lost the lot en route.

What a shame!

It was my own fault. Can't be helped.

In fact Gala's bag was stolen from the luggage compartment of a Mexican bus but there's no point in getting into that.

What about photos? Do you have any photos?

I didn't take a camera. I try to remember what's important.

Do you really? But how do you know what's important?

If I remember something, it's important.

Oh well, says her mother. Good to know your own mind, I suppose. I could get you some nice paper from the mill and you could draw what you remember.

I'm not drawing at the moment.

But for Dad – couldn't you draw some pictures for him?

I can't see what good that would do.

Anything's worth a try! says her mother, her voice thin, scratchy.

They are entering a drab little market town with close-packed streets, a dreary mix of rundown, post-war façades and cheap and cheerless makeovers. Gala hasn't passed this way since she was a child but little has changed: the window displays are dated and uninspired. The trading names are heavy on puns, alliteration and stating the obvious: Patty's Pie Pantry, Hairwaves, Message in a Bottle. The pavements are choked with young mums dragging truculent toddlers, heavy-set matrons rocking along with bulging supermarket bags as ballast, wizened grannies steering wobbly wheelie baskets around cracked slabs. Boozers jaw at The Cross. Crusty old boys walk hirpling dogs. Young blood props up the war memorial.

I thought we'd just go straight to see Dad.

Right now? I thought maybe – Gala smokes again, to stall her tongue.

What? What did you think?

I thought we could do that tomorrow.

But your father's expecting you. He's been expecting you for –

I'm just, well, I've been on the go for ages and I'm tired.

Tired? You're *tired?* Do you think I'm not tired? You haven't seen your father in all this time and you're wanting to put it off another day? I told him you were coming *today.* He does know the difference between one day and another, you know. He does have some perception of time, even if it's not quite the same as – He's expecting you. Looking forward to seeing you and he has precious little to look forward to. What am I to tell him now?

Okay, it's fine. Calm down, Mum, it's fine. We can go now, if you want.

Her mother grinds down a gear and the car jolts, causing the driver behind to brake sharply and lean on his horn.

I wouldn't want to *pressurise* you into going to see your father, whom you haven't seen for what – two years? – even though he's stuck in that godforsaken place and gets hardly any visitors. I certainly wouldn't want to do *that.*

I said it's fine. Let's go and see him. It's fine.

Gala puts a hand on her mother's shoulder, feels the silent judder of weeping. She hates it when her mother cries. And hates herself when she is the cause. But why does her mother have to cry so easily and so often?

Anyway, Gala says in her least confrontational voice, we've come this far already. No point in wasting petrol.

The town has tailed off to a straggle of low, terraced houses fringed by trees and fields. A smell of turnips wafts through the window, then manure, then something sweeter, toasted.

The porridge factory. We're nearly there.

Once again grinding the gears, her mother turns off the road and onto a long, tree-lined drive.

Your father will be so pleased to see you. By the way, even if he's up and about, he might still be wearing pyjamas. No need for alarm. And even if he doesn't *seem* pleased to see you or interested in what you say, he is really. He just doesn't always show it. Usually it's only me who comes to visit. And your brother, he's very good about visiting. When he can. He was hoping to be here today, to see you, but something came up.

I don't know what. He doesn't tell me much and when he does offer any information, I sometimes wish I hadn't asked. But he and I don't have much to say that your father hasn't heard before, whereas you must have so much to tell him. Of course you don't want to upset him. You must try not to upset your father.

After a bend in the drive, a large plain whitewashed building comes into view. Above the doorway, a large sign says: Welcome to The Pleasance. All Visitors Report to Reception.

Diving Through Fire

HER FATHER COULD dive through fire. That's what they said and Gala could picture him up on the dale, puffing out his fuzzy chest, sucking in his stomach, flexing skinny white legs as he worked up to the big finale. The dale was at the far end of the pool, a distance from the spectators' gallery and the changing rooms. Sixty-five clanging steel steps led to the concrete diving board. She knew how many steps because she'd counted as she climbed, then walked the length of the platform, peered over the edge, balked at the drop and, scaredy cat that she was, ignominiously retraced her steps.

For the spectators, no matter how sheltered a spot they thought they'd found on the peeling wooden benches, a sharp sea breeze slithered around the rocks and wormed through pullovers and windcheaters. They watched and waited. The pool attendant climbed part way up the diving tower and set a long, lit taper to the ring suspended between the top board and the water. Over from the west with his family, Miles Price, father of two, school teacher, weekend artist and, in the summer holidays, relief lifeguard, flexed his legs and extended his arms. The ring of fire flickered orange against a lavender dusk.

Already he had retrieved bricks and car keys from the bottom of the diving hole and with the aid of a rubber dummy, had demonstrated life-saving techniques. He had catapulted himself off the springboards into pikes and back flips and somersaults, but diving off the dale through a ring of fire would be his crowning moment.

The ring was a band of steel with kerosene-soaked rope wound round the frame and supported by two poles strapped to the central column. The flames danced in the light breeze. The ring quivered. As it had to be a tight enough fit to display skill and accuracy, to introduce an element of danger, the possibility of harm, it was not much bigger in circumference than a hula hoop. If there hadn't been a chance that the diver might have misjudged his angle of entry and scorched his skin, who'd have bothered to watch?

When he had fine-tuned his limbs and filled his lungs he took off, arcing upwards, jackknifing mid-air then stretching out and shooting clean through the flames. He entered the water with little more than a ripping sound like torn paper and a crown of bubbles gathering around the disappearing tips of his toes. Deep in the indigo pool, his plunging body hollowed out the curve of a boomerang. Applause rippled through the gallery. When he surfaced, climbed out and posed, Olympian, by the diving tower, the ring of fire flickered like the halo of a dark planet.

The thing is, Gala is not sure she really saw the show. She knows it happened because it was mentioned often, particularly by her father, and she can picture him, after the event, in drippy, droopy trunks, towel slung round his neck, eyebrows slightly singed. She can smell kerosene, scorched rope. As the crowd files out through the turnstile, he saunters towards the changing rooms, flushed with glory. As clear as can be, she can recall the dale, the sea beyond the pool wall rocking and slapping, and the distant lights of a fishing smack winking like a low-slung constellation. She can see the ring flickering against the deepening dusk but her father; did she really witness him diving through fire?

Walking on Water

SOMEHOW, THAT AFTERNOON, nobody was around. Stepping onto the pool wall in a still-dry swimsuit, Gala felt brave, bold. At the deep end the tide was already slopping over the wall. It was a big pool and, deserted, seemed bigger than ever. Beyond was a jag of rocks where a geyser of spume obscured the crumbling castle ruins. The castle was famous for its bottle dungeon. In the old days prisoners were dropped through the long, narrow bottleneck and fell to the bottom. It was said to be impossible to escape. Unless you could dig a tunnel through solid rock with an old bone.

Overhead, a gull swung through the damp grey air, crying and crying. As she made her way along the wall, arms outstretched like the tightrope walker she fancied she might be when she grew up. The heat of the veiled sun warmed the back of her neck. Walking on walls – the higher the better – was a favourite pastime. Whenever she got the chance she'd be up there, teetering, but a wall surrounded by air is nothing like one with sea slapping around. A little kick on the surface, an immense surge below.

The sky was still and heavy, the sea restless and heavy. Tensing her toes she stepped carefully, alert to slime and slither, crabs and jellyfish, anything which might cause her to squirm, to lose concentration, balance. She had to keep herself straight and steady, like a needle on a compass. A small fluctuation either way and she might be able to right herself but if she swung too wide of the mark she'd tip right over.

When the water was low enough to lap her ankles it was easy enough to stay upright, to become casual and confident, to allow her attention to wander. She compared the number of jellyfish wobbling out on the sea side to those in the pool. She charted the progress of clumps of seaweed and a bobbing turd. Which would be worse to come in direct contact with – jellyfish, turd or seaweed?

The tide was coming in quickly. With each step towards the deep end, the sea crept higher up her legs and soon she was setting her feet down on a wall she couldn't see. Safer to slow down but time with tidal pools is crucial: if she didn't push on, the tide would beat her back.

At the deep end, a chill came off the water and the rock and suck of the sea was far more menacing than she'd bargained for. Chittering, she looked back with longing to the shallow end, the paddling pool and the soft, safe, grassy bank. Where was everybody? Where was her father? Was her mother having an afternoon nap with her baby brother, in the boarding house which smelled of boiled eggs? Where was the man who looked after everything, fishing out muck and weed, netting the flotsam which sloshed in on the tide? And the lifeguard – wasn't there supposed to be a lifeguard on duty even if there was only one person who might need to be saved?

Gala's father had a certificate to prove he could swim with one arm while the other was wrapped around the person he was saving but he preferred diving demonstrations. Being a lifeguard, he said, was just a lot of standing around. But nobody was standing around, or even passing by on the esplanade. Was something happening on the other side of the hill which everybody, even Gran, had stopped to watch? Where was Gran?

It was too late now to remember that Gran had told her to keep clear of the water until she arrived. She was far from the warm shallows and grassy bank and had to keep going, to confront the stretch of wall where the tide was strongest and the water highest. Or go back the way she'd come and admit defeat. If she'd been able to swim more than a few frantic doggie paddles or sensible enough to put on the waterwings, which she'd left in the changing rooms, she could maybe have splashed back to the shallow end. Too late to be thinking about that now.

She took a deep breath, the way she'd seen her father do before he dived in and tunnelled underwater like a seal. She held the air in her puffed-out chest and high-stepped it, fast and anxious. The water was up to her knees. It knocked her about. Several times she almost missed her footing and the things she felt underfoot, hard, sharp things and slimy, squelchy things didn't matter a bit in the face of the great swaying, slapping mass of sea which could swallow her up and no-one would know, until somebody walking their dog or flying a kite came across her bloated body, washed up further down the coast; maggots and flies in the empty sockets of her eyes, hair tangled up in seaweed, crabs scuttling in and out of her decomposing mouth.

Stupid, stupid. Every time he took her swimming, her father drummed it into her that she must never go out of her depth. She'd get in trouble for this, for not paying attention, not doing what she was told, she'd get in so much trouble, get such a row, she'd be punished but whatever the punishment it couldn't be any more frightening than the sea all around, ready to swallow her whole. On the home stretch of submerged wall, she remembered to breathe again, drew in great gasps of air, concentrated on breathing deeply and not making a silly mistake. She'd already made one of those.

So as not to think about falling off the wall, she thought about lungs, how they inflated then deflated, how they couldn't stay filled, how the air would burst out if you tried to hold it in too long; the air had to be constantly changed, went in good, came out bad, you couldn't stop breathing in out in out, on and on or you'd turn red or purple or blue and die. Jas had been a blue baby. Almost strangled on his umbilicus.

Somehow all the thinking got her back safely to the shallow end and just as she reached the wide expanse of concrete, the sun broke through the clouds. She whooped and spun around. She'd done it! Safely back on solid ground, the sun was out, the sky blue, she whooped again and spun, high on bravery and boldness and relief – and then she was falling through sudden murky darkness, twisting, tumbling, drifting in no direction, time and space flowing slow and cold, the ringing in her ears as punishing as a dentist's drill – and then she was spitting and choking and retching, a hand was slapping her back and a voice, a dear, familiar voice was shouting:

Spit it oot, dearie, spit it oot!

Her eyes burned, throat burned, her chest, lungs, belly burned –

Spit it oot! spit it oot!

And Gala spat and gagged and retched up brine and bile. And when she was done, when her throat was raw and there was nothing more to bring up, Gran swaddled her in a towel, and hoisted her, gulping, onto her warm lap. Rocked her like a baby.

Gran's skirt and blouse were streaked with dark splashes. Her sandals were soaked through. Cream leather turned sludge brown.

Ye'll be the death o me, so ye will.

I got all the way round!

Whit in heaven's name were ye thinkin?

It was like being on a tightrope. In the circus.

I'll circus ye. Ye could've been a goner. Did I no tell ye tae save yir tricks till I got here? Dearie me, ye could've drooned! Just as well yir faither wisny here tae see me fishin ye oot. He'da strung me up! Made me walk the plank!

Gran filled a plastic mug with hot orange squash from the Thermos flask she brought to the beach come rain or shine.

Get this doon ye. And dinny gulp. Ye've done enough gulpin for yin day.

From her pocket, she magicked a dark disk wrapped in waxed paper. A treacle toffee.

Here. Awa and get yir claes on. Dry yourself properly. Mind and no choke on that chaw.

Gran sat herself down on the grassy slope next to the changing rooms and turned the toes of her wet sandals up to the sun.

The changing rooms were dank and smelly, rife with creepycrawlies and spiderwebs with throbbing, tormented knots at their centres. The stuff which usually bothered Gala, the sudden whirr of insect wings, the skewed scuttle underfoot, were nothing that day. When she had dried and dressed and shut the saloon-style door on the rotted wooden cubicle, she ran her dripping costume through the mangle and watched the seawater pour out of it.

By the time she was ready to leave, Gran's shoes had begun to lighten a shade or two and a salt crust was forming around the uppers. The tide was full in and it was impossible to determine where the pool ended and the sea began.

Back at the boarding house, where the Price family had taken two rooms for the fortnight, Gala pushed down leathery liver and charred onions without complaint. Gran gave her small, meaningful smiles across the table and said nothing at all about her reckless escapade at the swimming pool. That night, snug between crisp sheets and anchored by heavy, scratchy blankets, Gala dreamed she was a bell at the bottom of the sea.

Al Forno

HER FATHER PUT her head in the furnace. Well, not personally. He paid a man to do his dirty work for him. It had been raining in the night and the streets were still wet. He loaded the car with busts and heads and figurines – damp, pale, dead-looking things wrapped in veils of soggy muslin. Gala wore her favourite outfit: cherry red, jersey-knit trousers and a black and white dogtooth top. As it was still wet underfoot she also wore wellies, which rather spoiled the effect. Her mother had brushed her hair briskly and dragged it back with a clasp but hadn't had time to yank it into pigtails.

The car sat low on the road, a black bug which smelled of leather and petrol and the cigarettes her father enjoyed so much more when her mother wasn't around to complain about them. Being small, Gala's outlook was restricted to scarred, soot-black walls topped with barbed wire and broken glass, warehouses big enough to swallow whole towns, a speckled flurry of starlings and the tips of idle cranes.

The ships were the size of cathedrals. You might glimpse the bones of a massive skeleton crawling with hundreds of men or the slow passage of a dark hull slipping between the warehouses on the invisible river. On weekdays the hammering and the sizzling of welding torches never stopped and if you were passing at the end of the day, the lousing siren blared like a declaration of war and men flooded through the gates and onto the street, spreading out, breaking into fast-moving tributaries; heading home or to the pub.

But it was Sunday, the shipyard was silent and the gates bolted. When the landscape became even more abstract and impersonal and tramlines cats-cradled the road, Chitti's, which rarely shut on Sundays, was nearby. Was there a sign? Gala can only remember an opening, a gap in the wall, the tyres of the Austin squelching over mud.

In the courtyard, waves of heat flapped at her face. Had her father not been fully occupied with his clay models, she'd have taken his hand. Instead, shielding her eyes from the heat, she hung back. He cradled his box as if it were a baby or a cake, and would have been more upset about dropping it, and his work, than about his daughter taking a tumble, skinning her knees and spoiling her Sunday best.

Jas was too young to come to Chitti's, which made Gala feel important. Chitti's was exciting. Dangerous. Across the mud, through the archway, deep in the belly of the building, sparks flew and men in filthy singlets slid pieces of metal in and out of the furnace on long flat shovels. The furnace was much hotter than a baker's oven, hot enough for metal to melt and flow like a white-hot river.

The furnace was where Gala's head would go eventually but first it would be fired in a kiln. A mould would be made from the fired head and then something else would happen – her father had outlined the process but there were too many stages to remember – and some time later the head, which had started off as pale damp clay, would reappear as dark, lustrous bronze. Unbreakable. Everlasting. Which was also why she hung back. The heat haze bent the air. The foundrymen with big strong shoulders, smutty faces and sweat-shiny chests were scary, in a good way: sharp and thrilling. Her father had a spring in his step, which was also good, but that particular Sunday it wasn't good enough.

What's eating you? he asked.

Nothing.

Buck up, then.

It was unthinkable to say she didn't like the head, or the hairstyle. For the sitting, at her mother's insistence, and under her mother's muscular, piano-playing fingers, every strand of hair had been scraped back from her face, tightly braided and secured with nippy little elastic bands. As if loose, free hair was a sign of bad character.

Ah, Chitti! Good man. Hard at it, as ever?

As ever, Mr Price, aye. Time is money.

Chitti was special. At home, his name was spoken in a tone of respect. Chitti was needed, trusted.

Ciao, bella! But why no smile, *bambina?*

Where's your manners? said her father.

Manners, spanners, no matter manners. But so saaaaaad is baaaaad!

Manners was something Gala's parents cared a lot about. There was only one good set, like the electroplated nickel silver cutlery brought out for visitors; bright, shiny manners which involved *Please* and *Thank you* and *Speak when you're spoken to* and *Look at me when I'm talking to you* and *Don't mumble* and *Grownups know best.*

Chitti didn't care about manners but liked to see smiles. And if she was poker-faced, as she was that day, he'd lark about, do his best to draw a smile from her. Small, top heavy, with arms as long and strong as a gorilla, he hoisted her above his head, twirled her around three times then set her down and in his big, passionate voice belted out O *sole mil, sta n'fronte a te!* against the infernal racket of the foundry. She couldn't prevent a small smile from curling the corners of her mouth.

Dere, dere, da's better, *Bella!*

Bella meant beautiful. It was also the name of a large, lumbering girl who lived down the road from Gala and wasn't beautiful at all. *Ciao Bella* meant Hello Beautiful or Goodbye Beautiful. Chee aaaaaaaa ohhhhhhhh behhhhhhlllaaaaa. Those slow, viscous vowels flowing out of Chitti's throat were sweet as honey.

Her clay head would prove to anybody who saw it –

and people would be able to go on seeing it all through her childhood, womanhood, her old age, even after she was dead the proof would be there for anybody to see – that *Bella* was not an accurate description: she had fat, ugly pigtails; the sulk made her eyebrows buckle like hairy caterpillars and her lips press together like rubber suckers. Even so, the word *Bella* glistened inside her own, flesh and blood head.

In preparation to leave, her father and Chitti went through their customary rigmarole:

A lot on at the moment, Chitti?

Oh yes, very busy, Mr Price.

No rest for the wicked.

Or da good, hardworking man, sir. I dunno where da time goes.

Are you suggesting a long wait is likely?

No no, sir. I say I do for you, so I do.

Glad to hear it.

Except for da unseen circumstance, sir.

Let's hope we have none of that! Well, I'd better let you get on. Strike while the iron's hot, heh, heh!

Right you are, Mr Price. *Ciao,* sir. *Ciao Bella*!

The pigtails and sulk were handed over for Chitti to work his hot, dirty magic and preserve them forever. As Gala's head changed hands, she made a wish: a selfish, destructive wish involving the explosive combination of stray air bubbles, hard-packed clay and high temperatures. She flushed at the badness of it but with all the shimmering, distorting heat around, nobody noticed the guilty pinkness of her cheeks.

In With the Freaks

SHE'D SLEPT IN, was running late and her parents didn't like to be kept waiting. When they'd phoned to arrange the visit, they'd suggested picking her up at the flat:

We won't stay long, her mother said. We won't pry.

Gala stalled them, arranged to meet at the National Portrait Gallery. No way were they coming to her current residence, where by accident more than design – it was cheap, she was desperate – she was in with the freaks.

As always the kitchen was a cool, freaky tip. CarolAnn's fetish gear was mixed up with baby stuff, dope doings and Genius Jake's ever-growing collection of fertility goddesses. CarolAnn, wearing nothing but a skimpy black slip, was slouched in the high-backed rattan chair, breastfeeding Rainbow Suzi.

Hey, she said, looked up momentarily, then slid her heavy-lidded eyes back to the huge baby gobbling at her tiny maternal breast. As always, CarolAnn gave off an aura of spaced, superior boredom. At the other end of the kitchen table, a guy Gala had never seen before was reading a beat-up copy of *Thus Spake Zarathustra*, fondling a rampant ginger beard and contemplating CarolAnn's vacant breast.

Hi, said Gala.

Hey, he replied, then returned his attention to Nietzsche and CarolAnn.

Rainbow Suzi's shitty nappies were soaking in a tub and stinking out the kitchen. A squadron of empties – Southern Comfort, Jose Cuervo tequila and Newcastle Brown Ale – had colonised a large portion of the kitchen floor.

Dead men, man, said the beardy guy. Dead men standing.

The bin was bulging. In the vegetable rack carrots were growing their own beards and mushrooms were composting themselves.

Breakfast options. Option. Muesli. There was always muesli. The freaks ate the stuff at any time of day or night. CarolAnn subsisted on muesli, alfalfa sprouts and heroin, which kept her waif-like and irresistible to men. There was no milk. No juice. No coffee. No bread, cheese, oatcakes. In the fridge was a glass jar which contained one dill pickle suspended in what looked like pondwater, and two eggs on which somebody had written in felt tip: EAT ME AND DIE. A solitary tea bag lay at the bottom of a rusty caddy. Just the other day Gala had bought a box of fifty, on special offer. Not much of a bargain after all.

Man, this place is honking.

It was Genius Jake, bringing into the kitchen his own honk of unwashed clothes. Though Jake took frequent, lengthy baths – he liked to soak and chant mantras, and fancy he was raising himself onto a higher plane of consciousness – he considered it too much hassle to launder his lumberjack shirts and elephant cords.

Genius Jake was so called because he had rigged the electricity meter so the pad had free, unlimited, illegal power, and because he could string sentences together long after everybody else had succumbed to a dope-induced stupor. The previous night, temple balls and Thai sticks had been doing the rounds and Gala's brain felt like a sock stuffed down the back of a mouldering couch.

What's up, kid? said Jake. You look so totally straight today.

Meeting the parents.

Gala was wearing the skirt and jacket, tan tights and sensible shoes she normally reserved for job interviews, which, she hoped, gave as little away about her lifestyle as possible.

Bummer, said Jake. You should take 'em to Fat Kitty's. Blow their mind.

Fat Kitty's was the scene: so laid back it was horizontal. The décor had been thrown together from stuff salvaged from skips and bins, liberated from bourgeois patios, picked up at jumble sales, begged, borrowed or ripped off. Only freaks frequented the place. Nobody else had the time to wait. Service happened if and when, slugs in the salad were considered added protein by the few carnivores amongst the clientele. If Fat Kitty, a gangly, temperamental transvestite, reckoned you didn't pass the dress code – ragbag chic – or might in some other way blow the vibe of the place, he'd retrieve the pet rat from his padded bra and let it scamper from his scrawny neck to a big, bony foot. It was an effective strategy for getting rid of uncool customers.

You done with that tea bag? said Jake. Can I give it a squeeze?

Help yourself.

CarolAnn switched Rainbow Suzi from one breast to the other.

Yeah, man, she drawled, I gotta do some, like, *shopping* today but I'm, like, waiting on a guy who owes me to show. A drag, man. Anybody got any bread?

My pockets are empty, honey chile, but my heart is full.

Yeah, right, said CarolAnn, allowing the merest flicker of a smile to intrude on her expression of supreme boredom. What about the kid. Got any bread, kid?

Man and woman cannot live by bread alone, said Jake.

I'm totally skint, said Gala.

Thought you were, like, working? said CarolAnn.

I am, but it's two weeks' lie time before I get paid.

Lie time?

CarolAnn didn't know much about legit work. On how to claim benefits, how to wheedle and inveigle and make a nice little profit from drug dealing and other unspecified services, CarolAnn was a sage.

A drag, man, she said. Rainbow Suzi needs macrobiotic rusks, new Babygros –

I mean, like, see how this baby *grows*, yeah – and cream for her bum. She's got like this totally freaky nappy rash.

As CarolAnn wasn't hitting on the bearded guy for bread, it was likely they were having some sort of scene.

Gala wasn't fooled. CarolAnn never paid for rusks or baby bum cream. She ripped that stuff off, using the baby as a decoy and stuffing the pram with loot. Bread, her own and whoever else's she could get her hands on, was for strictly personal necessities.

Her parents were waiting restlessly at the entrance to the gallery. Her father, in a stormtrooper's cap and buckskin flying jacket, was puffing and pacing. Her mother, with a strained smile, was checking the street in both directions.

Hello dear! Is that all you're wearing? Don't you have a coat? It's a cold wind. Aren't you cold? There's so much grit in the wind. And the streets are not nearly as clean as they used to be. When we lived here –

There you are, said her father. You're late.

I know. Sorry. I ran all the way.

We could have picked you up, he grumbled. I told you that.

It would have been nice to see where you live, said her mother.

Another time, said Gala. Cool cap, Dad.

But no, you wanted to have it your way.

Gala's here now, Miles. That's all that matters, isn't it?

Throughout the reunion, two gallery attendants in tartan trews and blazers, one tall and saturnine with a twelve o'clock shadow, the other short and plum-cheeked, stood to attention. As they were about to make for the exhibition room, the tall attendant, in lugubrious tones, addressed Gala's father:

Would you care to leave your coats in the cloakroom?

That won't be necessary. We won't be staying long.

Very good, sir.

Nevertheless, the plum-cheeked one added, there is an entrance fee of two pound per person.

An entrance fee? For an exhibition?

This is the National Portrait Gallery, sir. The ticket price goes towards the upkeep of our collection which is costly to maintain but, as I'm sure you understand, a most valuable asset to the nation.

Better be good, then, her father growled and slapped his cash on the counter.

Thank you, sir. Enjoy the exhibition.

At the price, I certainly hope to.

The hushed corridors leading to the main gallery were dimly lit and deeply carpeted. The walls were sage green and lined with gloomy old oil paintings of famous patriarchs.

Well, this is nice, said her mother. Nice to see you again, at last. Though you're looking awfully pale. Are you eating properly? Dad, don't you think Gala is looking pale? Dad, I was saying –

I heard you. Yes, she's looking pale. She always looks pale. It's her natural colouring.

Yes, Miles, but don't you think she's paler than usual?

How would I know when we haven't seen her in months?

I had a late night, that's all. What's been happening with you two?

Oh not a lot, her mother replied.

Not a lot you need to know about, said her father. Nothing worth mentioning.

Your dad did have a little *turn* –

Do you get my drift, Vera? *Nothing worth mentioning*!

Her mother sighed bleakly but held her tongue.

So what are your plans for the summer? her father asked.

I've fixed up a job at the breweries.

The breweries? But you've just graduated! What sort of job's that for a graduate?

It's good money.

And what do you intend to do after the summer?

I don't know. I was thinking about going to Europe.

To do what?

I'm not sure. Just to see somewhere else, another country. See how others live.

What in hell's name is the point of that?

I do wish we could have seen your flat, said her mother. Dad and I used to have digs down your way. Just a few streets away. We were looking on the map, weren't we, Miles? Our landlady was forever complaining about me practising the piano, wasn't she? What was her name again, Dirndl? Dingle?

Vera looked to Miles for acknowledgement, agreement, some fond memory of their shared past.

I can't remember what some landlady from thirty years ago was called. And Gala's not interested in hearing about her.

I don't mind.

It's ancient history, he insisted. Dead and gone.

Her mother smiled bravely, and continued:

We were thinking of the George Hotel for lunch. Your father worked there as a waiter when he was at Art College but the menu looked awfully dear.

The entrance to the exhibition was up ahead. A bright, undulating banner carried the title: *New Directions in Portraiture*.

Here we are! Gala said, trying to sound enthusiastic, though she'd have happily had an excuse to go back to bed. The exhibition got a good review in *The Guardian*.

The Guardian? said her father. You don't mean to tell me you read that pinko rag?

The Guardian's based in Manchester isn't it? her mother chirped. Isn't it, Miles?

As it was previously called *The Manchester Guardian*, one would assume as much.

In the sudden bright light of the exhibition room Vera flushed and tucked her chin into the folds of a peacock blue scarf.

Nice scarf, Mum. Suits you.

It was a present from Beattie McCord. For no reason! Don't you think that's extravagant, giving somebody a present for no reason?

What's wrong with it?

Her mother sighed, bit her lip.

We've only just met and already you're disagreeing with me. How's Jas?

Fine, said her father.

Well, he's had a bit of trouble with –

He's fine, said her father. Least said, soonest mended.

Her father strode around the gallery at speed; arms folded, brows knitted. He approached each exhibit warily, as if it might leap up and bite him, then spun on his heels, emitting ejaculations of exasperation, incredulity, bafflement, disgust.

The works bore little relation to traditional portraiture, to subjects posed comfortably and looking pensive. Traditional materials were in short supply. Instead, the artists had used plastic, polystyrene, papier mâché, crushed tin cans, foam rubber, sweetie papers, congealed porridge.

One piece, entitled *Adolf,* was a cairn of old shoes stuffed with swastikas and joke shop moustaches. Another consisted of a greengrocer's barrow filled with coconuts. Each coconut had a label which, on closer inspection, turned out to be a caricature of Grocer Heath. Her mother tutted.

That's not a portrait, said her father, that's an insult.

I think it's meant to be making a point, Dad. This artist is known for his satirical work.

The trouble is, he continued, nobody these days knows how to *use paint.* Art has to have some aesthetic appeal, to show some *technique.*

I don't know anything about art, said her mother breezily, but I don't get this stuff. I just don't get it.

I get it all right, said her father, it's a bunch of wiseguys cocking a snook at the powers that be. Any idiot can do that.

Keep your voice down, Miles, said her mother.

What for? There's nobody else here! he said, louder still. And no bloody wonder. If I were you, Gala, I wouldn't waste my time gawping at tosh like this. You'd learn more from chimpanzees let loose in a junkyard.

Scientists have discovered that chimps are much more intelligent than we thought, said Gala. I was reading about a place in Russia where –

If you want to take your lead from commie chimpanzees, don't let me stop you.

Come on, Miles, said her mother. Let's go and have lunch. You'll be in a better frame of mind after you've eaten.

What do you mean? What's wrong with my frame of mind? What exactly are you insinuating?

Vera made to take his arm and guide him towards the exit. He brushed her hand away and strode on alone, leaving Gala and her mother to trail after him and, under the inscrutable gaze of the gallery attendants, attempt to effect a civilised exit.

Barras

SHE COULD SMELL the place from the far end of the street –
chips and vinegar, fried onions and toffee apples, sour sweat
and fusty tweed, tobacco and mothballs, the petroleum whiff
of plastic macs. Traders barked their wares and fired off round
after round of wisecracks. In the thick of the stalls, standing at
half the height of the grownups – amid the buzz of cash-only
transactions and the crammed mass of folk hot for a bargain –
was like being inside a human hive.

Going to the Barras wasn't shopping in the way that going for
messages with Gran or, less often, her mother, meant. That was
queuing in the butcher's, jammed up against carcasses of cows,
sheep and pigs hung from ceiling hooks; or the greengrocer's,
where brass scales tipped beneath pyramids of apples, bananas,
onions and beets. That kind of shopping was about waiting
your turn, getting what you came for.

Gran always had a friendly word for the shopkeeper during
her purchase of braising beef, stewing mutton, a ham bone, a
pound of carrots, and would happily pass the time with whoever
stood next to her in the queue. It was mostly women who did
the shopping. A man with a message basket over his arm was a
bachelor, a 'bachelor', a widower, or a husband whose wife was
too sick to attend to her duties.

Gala's mother didn't go in for food queue conversation. If

another customer tried to engage her in chit-chat about the weather, the price of butter, how lucky they were to be this side of the Iron Curtain, what she thought of the Cuban situation or the American Civil Rights Movement, her response was curt. And if she did find herself next to one of her chums, she wouldn't want the whole shop overhearing a personal exchange, would she?

The Barras was nosing around: a poke here, a rummage there, no guarantee of finding anything usable but who knows what might turn up under a heap of junk. The price had to be right, that is cheap: a bargain, a steal. Some vendors tried to catch the attention of each and every passerby. Others ignored the punters – or pretended to – until a definite purchase was in the offing. In the meantime they chin-wagged with neighbouring stallkeepers and puffed heartily on Capstan Full Strength, Player's Navy Cut, Craven A.

The Barras was somewhere else she and her father went without Jas. He was too little, the place too busy. It would have been easy to lose a small child in the crush of humanity. At first, Gala's father was easy-going, almost patient, inching through the dense crowds, his hand intermittently reaching out for hers. When something caught his eye, he'd pause, pick it up. Old stuff caught his eye, though pretty much everything at the Barras was old. He favoured hard, heavy things: tools, pots, weapons. When he was particularly interested, he'd narrow his eyes, which he did when he was working on a sculpture, as if shrinking his field of vision helped him see more clearly.

Preferring the bright and shiny, the soft and floaty, Gala tried to interest him in a length of purple velveteen.

It would make a great magician's cloak.

That's as may be, he said. But not what I'm looking for.

What are you looking for?

Inspiration, he said. Inspiration.

He paid little attention to fabrics though once in a while, if he was in a painting phase, he might cast an eye over a paisley-patterned pashmina or embroidered mantilla.

Might do for background colour, he'd say.

For Gala, the man who sold magic tricks was the main

attraction. He didn't have a stall but moved around, setting up a quick demonstration then moving on, never stopping anywhere for long. Like a true magician, he could vanish at the drop of a hat and reappear somewhere else. Artful Arcady, he called himself.

While her father inspected a dull jug – Stoneware, he said, an unusual glaze – she sidled up to a stall selling crystal paperweights which appeared to have real flowers trapped inside the glass. How they were made was something to puzzle over, like a ship in a bottle. But there was something dead about the flowers trapped inside glass so she turned her attention to a stinky stall which sold kittens and puppies.

As yet, there were no pets in the Price household. Did she want a pet? When her mother wasn't around to shake a broom at them for doing their business in the bushes, cats prowled the back garden, wings and tails of half-eaten birds poking out of their mouths. Cats hissed and spat and scratched. Dogs barked and drooled, snarled and snapped. Some dogs bit people. Gala didn't think she wanted a cat or a dog. A rabbit, or a dove which could pop out of a top hat, that might have been a pet worth having.

She wasn't meant to stray far. The place rambled and doubled back on itself. It would be easy to slip out of sight amongst the big bellies and broad beam ends, the floppy breasts and sweaty armpits. Just as she was giving up hope of any magic that day, she caught sight of a shiny buckle on a cracked leather belt, green buckskin trousers and yes, the gold earring, the oiled curls, the red polka-dot neckerchief.

Dad. Dad!

Her father was inspecting yet another pot, turning the dull, brick-coloured vessel around, checking for chips or flaws in the glaze.

Can we watch the magic tricks? Please!

This could be a find. This could be an antique!

Arcady will be gone in a minute.

What on earth are you on about?

Artful Arcady.

Who?

The man who sells magic tricks.

Oh him. Magic my foot. He's a con man, more like.

He'll be gone in a minute.

A good thing too. A shifty character, that one. Tinker. Itinerant. Wouldn't trust him as far as I could throw him. Stay where I can see you, d'you hear?

He turned the pot over, scrutinised the marks on the bottom. Gala squeezed through the crowd, drawn by the voice which twanged like a plucked string.

Floomox yeer freends, liedees and gints, bemboozle them wey yeer sloight oov hend.

Arcady didn't look like a magician – no cloak or wand, no top hat or rabbits – more like a gypsy or a pirate, the frilly shirt open at the neck, the striped waistcoat with shiny buttons, the thick bands of silver on his fingers.

Neow yee see it, neow yee dun't. Kent beloive yeer oyes?

Between one swift hand and another, he arced the cards back and forth, made a whirring fan of them hang in mid-air. Folk began to gather round in anticipation of a show. Arcady kept up the patter, worked the crowd.

Her father liked card games. Well, he liked bridge, which went on for hours and looked boring. Her mother always seemed to have organ practice on bridge nights, so a couple and another man or woman would come to the house to make up a foursome. The players sat on and on, laying their cards on the table, sipping beer or whisky – or both – and smoking. When they reached the end of one game, there would be a flurry of coughs and guffaws. More cigarettes would be lit, more drink poured. And on it would go until the bridge players put on their coats and went home, noisier than they had come in. Gala can't remember who the other players were. Except one.

She was meant to be asleep long before the game was done but sometimes she got out of bed and sat on the stairs, in the hope of hearing or seeing something interesting. Usually it was the same old stuff but one night, just as she was losing interest, she caught sight of her father helping a woman into her coat.

By itself this was nothing unusual. A gentleman was expected to help a lady put on her coat, to open doors for her, carry her suitcases, as if women were incapable of performing any of these simple tasks for herself. The woman in question had shiny black hair and orange lipstick, a bit like Nana Mouskouri without the spectacles. She was smoking a black cigarette with a gold tip. It wasn't the first time the woman had been her father's bridge partner. After he had performed his gentlemanly duty with the coat, she pressed her chest against his and said slurrily:

Button me up nice and tight, Miles. Wouldn't want me catching my death, would you?

Rosetta, he said, his voice deep and rumbly, like a car in low gear. Ah, Rosetta. No, I would not want that. Heaven forbid, Rosetta.

Gala had crept back to bed, pulled the covers over her head and listened hard until the front door closed, Rosetta's heels clipped up the path and the gate swung shut. She doesn't remember her mother coming home.

There you are! her father snapped, yanking her away from Arcady's fan of cards. What did I tell you? Wandering off without so much as a by your leave. Just like everybody else. Wandering off. Leaving me in the lurch.

Just as Arcady was about to reveal the secret of a new trick, her father marched her off and made her stand beside him in front of a messy pile of weapons: knives, swords, cutlasses, pistols, revolvers, flintlocks, rifles, shotguns. Most were dull with tarnish and rust but here and there was a glint of silver or brass, a pale inlay of ivory or mother-of-pearl. He picked up a double-barrelled shotgun, inspected the detail on the decorative handle, ran his palm down the barrels, flicked back the catch, took aim and pretended to fire into the air. The big, saggy stallkeeper stuck a finger through a hole in his jersey and scratched his belly.

I doubt anybody'd hit much with this, said her father.

Could still gie somebody a scare, said the man. That's whit maitters, is it no?

Her father put down the gun and picked up a small dagger with a strange, wavy blade.

Keris, he said, holding it up for inspection. Haven't seen one of these in a long time.

The dagger glinted in a kind of tired way, as if too many men like her father had held it up to the light. He stared intently at the keris for a long time, as if he were seeing something entirely different, as if he were somewhere entirely different, in a faraway place not a bit like the Barras or Glasgow or anywhere Gala had ever been.

The names of faraway places drifted around the Price household: Kenya, Uganda, Tanganyika, Siam, Ceylon, Java. Sometimes letters arrived. Gala's mother steamed off the stamps, which often featured big game: lions, tigers, elephants, wildebeests, rhinoceroses, and stuck them in her *Movaleaf Illustrated, loose leaf STAMP ALBUM of postage stamps of the world*. It was a thick, heavy album with a stiff, red canvas jacket and a green, embossed title. The letters had a connection with the faraway part of Gala's father, especially the letters from Java, where tea and coffee grew and bad things had happened. To Granny and Grandad Price, whom she hardly knew.

Tcha! Tcha! Tcha! Her father jabbed the air with the keris. I'll give you a quid for it, he told the stallkeeper.

You're haein me on, guv. That's worth a tenner at least. Rarity value.

Her father held the dagger high then cut a swathe through the air.

Hear that? he said. That's a dull note. A good keris sings. This is an inferior piece. Practically worthless.

I could dae it for seven.

Purely decorative. No function as a weapon. Ten a penny at source. If I gave you a quid for it, I'd be doing you a favour.

It's an antique, so it is. Hails fae the Far East. Near where yon stoater o a volcano erupted. Krakatoa, aye. *Krakatoa, East o Java.*

You don't need to tell me where the bloody thing's from, said her father, tossing the knife on the table and calling it a day.

Bohemians

ON THE FIRST floor landing of the Price house stood a life-sized statue of a naked man. He was green and had a sleek, muscular frame, a blank gaze and a few decorative curls on his cast metal head; between his legs an emblematic penis was also surrounded by a few curls. Real men had more hair than the green man. Gala's father didn't have much on his head but he did have a scratchy black moustache and dark scribbles on his chest and legs, and in his armpits. When he was wet from swimming or the bath, the hairs would straggle down his body like seaweed dragged by the current.

Most of the time, the green, unusually fine figure of a man stood unnoticed, gazing out – if you could gaze with eyes which lacked pupils and irises – across the landing, towards the bathroom. On Patience nights, when Auntie Win, or Lil – who weren't really aunties but Gran's old lady friends – came to visit, Gala's mother suddenly remembered the green man and covered up his private parts with a bath towel. For modesty's sake, she said. His right arm, bent at the elbow in front of the rippling washboard of his diaphragm, made a convenient towel rail. The draped nude, as her father described the effect, took on an air of mystery he somehow lacked in the altogether.

On Patience nights, a felt-topped card table was unfolded and set up in the front room. The bell would ring and the door would open to one smiling old lady or another, standing on the doorstep, clutching a handbag and smiling cheerily. The old ladies, who came separately and together, brought in a breath of the city, of the dark glittering racket of the starlings in George Square and the sooty fug of close-packed tenements. They wore wool coats which, like them, had seen better days and worse, felt hats pinned to thinning hair – or in Win's case, to her salt and pepper wig – sparkly brooches, densely powdered noses and intense, startling shades of lipstick.

While the old ladies adjusted cardies and patted shampoo-and-sets into place, it was Gala's job to hang up the coats and hats. Win was tall and bony, with horsey dentures and a face as ridged and sallow as a walnut. Her wig had a habit of slipping. Lil was a wee old peach, with soft, fuzzy cheeks. Once they had smoothed out the creases in their skirts, they dug into handbags and brought out treats for the wee ones. When Jas was very little they brought chocolate buttons, fruit jellies and bendy black discs of liquorice. When he could be trusted to sook safely they brought hard, long-lasting sweeties: soor plooms, pineapple cubes, mint humbugs. They'd never have dreamed of coming empty-handed.

Neither Lil nor Win had grandchildren of their own, or indeed children, to indulge. Lil had never married and Win, like Gran – Lottie to her friends – was widowed so young and so soon after marriage, she had no time to start a family. Gran herself was a widow before she gave birth and her friends referred to Vera, much to Vera's mortification, as 'poor Lottie's posthumous daughter'.

There was a set order to Patience nights. Gran would lead her guests to the front room where they would each partake of a small sherry in the good crystal glasses, accompanied by a single cigarette. The three friends had lived through the first and the second war with Germany; frugality seasoned with a dash of recklessness was in their blood. They sipped and smoked and compared notes on the health of a shrinking circle of friends and relatives. Sherry was followed by tea, Russian tea with lemon, served in tall glasses with metal frames, and a nice slice of fruit cake. And then it was the cards: Patience, Canasta,

Pelmanism, Gin Rummy. There was never any actual gin.

On Patience nights, as well as checking on Jas from time to time, though in those days the kid slept well, Gala's job was to fetch and carry for the card players. More often than not, Lil or Win would tip her a silver sixpence for her trouble. If her friends were short that month, Gran would dig into her own battered purse. When she wasn't required, Gala would sit on the hall stairs, masticating her way through a bag of sweeties, a few steps down from the green man, draped for the benefit of Win and Lil. Not that the old ladies were easily offended. Even when the whole house could hear Miles curse because he'd hit his thumb with a hammer or dropped a chunk of stone on his toes, they prattled on brightly. Never loud, never raucous. And never a word of complaint. Old ladies who knew their place, counted their blessings, made the best of things with their tinkling, silvery laughter.

Gala's mother and father were the ones who took offence about obscure, intangible instances of insult: the look on her face, her tone of voice, a whole spectrum of perceived behaviour which they interpreted, rightly or wrongly, as impertinence, insolence, downright rudeness. How could a statue give offence? When her father first lugged the green man up the stairs and set him on the landing, Vera pronounced him *indecent*.

A naked man in full view of all comers. What will people think, Miles?

It's a *nude*, her father replied. How many times do I have to tell you? And it's staying where it is. It's one of my best pieces.

Well, really, Vera sniffed. Do you want people to think we're bohemians?

As a rule, grownups didn't stand around in the buff. Gala had seen Jas in the bath and wondered why he had a fat little sprinkler and she didn't. Once or twice, also in the bath, she'd caught sight of her mother's unclothed body, her big blue-white breasts bobbing on the surface of the bathwater like eggs in a frying pan, the dark nest of hair between her legs. She'd seen her father in swimming trunks and pyjama bottoms but never in the altogether.

The green man looked more like a Greek god than any flesh-and-blood bloke you might bump into on the streets. Not that it was customary to see a naked man of any kind on the streets, or even one in what might be described as a state of undress. In high summer a man might carry his jacket over his arm, he might roll up his shirtsleeves or loosen his collar but that was about it. Except for the coalman, who wore a sleeveless vest, sackcloth trousers and boots, whatever the weather. Or the scoutmaster, who wore shorts and knee-length socks, to be like the boys.

Gala's father must have seen many naked/nude/bare people. He must have looked closely at them, narrowed his eyes and squinted to see more clearly. He must have spent long periods of time getting to know all the details of their bodies. Who had been the models for his sketches and statues? Was there really a man who looked like a Greek god somewhere in Glasgow? Would Gala recognise him if she passed him on the street? And what about the ladies with arms above their heads and long, wavy hair cascading down their backs? Who were they and where had they taken off their clothes for her father? And why had he wanted to make sketches and statues of people without their clothes on? Was there something wrong with him? What was a bohemian?

Waterwings

ON SUNDAY MORNINGS when he didn't have heads, busts or figurines needing to be delivered to the foundry and Gala's mother was committed to pulling out the stops, depressing the foot pedals and hammering the fingerboard of a church organ in Yoker, her father took Gala and her pot-bellied, chubby-cheeked brother to the baths. They must have gone any number of times to the baths but only one specific memory remains.

The choppy water was an opaque, snot green. The building was old and crumbling; patches of paintwork had bubbled into mouldy growths which resembled burnt popcorn.

Voices swelled and leapt about, bent as they hit the walls and bounced back. A glass-panelled roof offered a glimpse of outside, of the time of day, the weather. At the shallow end stood deep ceramic sinks for washing and warming up. A row of hissing wall taps splashed into the sinks. The water was tepid, warm at best, never properly hot.

Neither Gala nor Jas could swim without the support of a rubber ring, waterwings, or their father's arms and his loudly repeated instructions: *In through the nose, out through the mouth.*

Miles could swim the whole length of the pool underwater. He didn't seem human when he swam, more like a torpedo programmed to move directly towards its target, forcing all

47

obstacles out of its path. Other dads were the same, each carving out his own channel in the water. They didn't stop, didn't move to the side, look around; even at the shallow end where tots splashed and squealed, the serious swimmers just crashed on and everybody else had to get out of the way.

On Sunday mornings it was mostly dads and kids at the baths. Mums went to church then prepared Sunday lunch: they wrapped a roast in dripping or basted a chicken, peeled spuds, scrubbed carrots, shelled peas, made bread sauce or gravy. There was soup for mothers to think about as well, and pudding. People had great expectations of Sunday lunch. And if you'd been to the baths in the morning, you were hungrier than ever.

The few women who went to the pool tended to go alone. They wore bathing caps embossed with rubber flowers. Mostly they swam breaststroke, and Gala assumed for long enough that the name of the swimming style was related to female anatomy. When Jas was able to attempt any kind of stroke, he would not swim breaststroke. Men did the crawl, the back crawl or the lolloping butterfly, which was closer in motion to a walrus hoisting itself onto a rock than that of the prettiest, most delicate of creatures.

While her father was doing his lengths, Gala was in charge of Jas, who was still so small that even in the shallow end, he was out of his depth. Miles had given Gala a lesson, the same lesson as the previous time. He'd thrown Jas in the air a few times, dunked him to get him used to shutting his mouth underwater, popped him into the ring and left her to it. The rubber ring was too big for Jas. He was forever slithering through it and Gala had to drag him back up to the surface, blinking and spluttering.

Her plan that day had been to get as close to the deep end as possible before being apprehended by the lifeguard. She knew *how* to swim. She'd learnt the basics of the breaststroke: *up, out, together, breathe in, pull with the arms, push with the legs, breathe out,* but hadn't yet plucked up the courage to take off the pink rubber waterwings and so was officially confined to bobbing about in the shallow end. But plittering about the shallow end was boring. Her father had said he'd only be five minutes but thirteen had already gone by on the wall clock and anyway, once his head was down and he was into his lengths, how would he know how long he'd been swimming?

Gala must have bribed Jas with sweets, a ha'penny from her pocket money or the green plastic spaceman which came free in the Cornflakes packet. Whatever it was, the bribe had done the trick: her wee brother had promised to sit safely on the steps at the shallow end while she struck out for the deep end.

It was going fine. The water was becoming gradually colder which meant deeper. She couldn't see the lifeguard which meant that he couldn't see her. *Up, out, together, breathe in, pull with the arms, push with the legs, breathe out.* She was making headway but the waterwings didn't seem as buoyant as usual. She was about halfway down the pool and just beginning to get out of her depth when, from the poolside, she heard rapid pattering. Jas, in wrinkled turquoise trunks, was scampering towards the deep end, as fast as his wee legs would carry him. Which was a lot faster than she was moving through the water.

The monkey – he'd promised to sit on the steps and wait until she'd got back! She yanked herself along the rail.

Slow down! Stop! Go back! You'll fall! You'll crack your head open, get concussion! You'll get a row, a really big row!

Heedless, with no thought of future repercussions in his two-year-old brain, Jas steamed on. At the deep end he clambered onto a diving block, lowered his curly head, thrust out his skinny arms and kicked off into a near-perfect dive.

Dragging herself along the rail towards the deep end, Gala yelled the length of the pool:

Dad! Dad!

Her voice was lost in the din. At the shallow end her father was hoisting himself out of the water and heading for the hot tubs. Blind to her, deaf to her.

Dad! Dad!

Jas had surfaced and was bobbing and blinking and flapping his arms. Giggling. Fearless. She clung to the rail and yelled, really yelled for her father, as Jas once again went under.

Where was the lifeguard? Could nobody see the tot at the deep end? Or his sister, way out of her depth, in waterwings which felt as deflated as her lungs and who couldn't reach him without letting go of the rail? The water was deep, the waterwings must have a puncture, they were hissing. Could she learn to swim and lifesave at the same time? Would she drown in the process?

DAAAADDD!

What use was a lifeguard who told you off for shrieking and dive-bombing when you were perfectly safe and doing nobody any harm and then, when you were out of your depth and your brother was sinking, was nowhere to be seen?

DAAAAAAAADDD!

Somehow her father, and several other men, turned and stared down the length of the pool, hand to brow, like they were searching the distant horizon for sight of land. When Miles Price spotted his children – his daughter dithering between clinging to the rail and striking out in the hope of reaching her brother, his son bobbing and dipping – he dropped into the pool, took a breath, a very deep breath, threw himself forward and tunnelled towards them, somehow reaching the deep end in time to lunge, sweep his children into his arms and plonk them both, spitting and wailing on the steps. Miles the hero.

A Lack of Faith

GALA WENT TO an island. Was sent. Alone. On a ferry, a steamer, that much is certain: the big funnel, the deep underfoot shudder from the engine room. Did she travel to the coast by train or is the memory of sitting in a wood-trimmed compartment next to Gran, dressed in her stepping-out best – a tailored navy suit, a cream blouse and felt hat – out of synch? She remembers a steam train near the end of the era of steam – a man shovelling coals into a brazier, the shrill whistle, the scratchy upholstery which chafed the backs of her knees, whooshing blasts misting up the windows, the soporific shoogle.

If Gran accompanied her to the coast, she didn't come on the ferry, so what did she do – take a turn on the prom then catch another train back to town? Visit a friend who'd left the city grime for soothing views from the Clyde coast? Gala would have scampered up the gangplank and waved as the ferry pulled away from the quay. Was the crossing rough? One thing is certain: she'd have been up on deck, on the topmost deck, leaning out from the rail, tilting her face to the fine salty spray, letting her hair, freed from kirby grips and rubber bands, whip and tangle and slap her face.

If she'd had a piece, she'd have thrown the crusts to the gulls. She'd have walked all the way round the deck, time and again, swaying with the swell, working on her sea legs. She'd have

watched as the houses and factories on the mainland shrank
into a toytown, made herself dizzy staring into the ferry's wake
where the foam stitched itself into a broad train of rippling lace.

After the deep grinding from the engine room and the ferry
swinging round and lining up with the quay, she'd have skipped
down the gangplank. She'd have felt out of kilter from once
again walking on solid ground and, perhaps, from being met
by the many McCords. Lou McCord was a lanky man with a
thatch of oat-coloured hair who could smile and frown at the
same time. His wife Beattie was broad-hipped and brisk. Always
a baby on the breast, at the hip or on the way. Beattie's mother,
Mrs Wellsley, was on the island, as were all the children: Ailsa,
Iona, Col, Skye and baby Harris. As Gala was closest in age to
Ailsa, whenever their mothers met to take tea and blether, the
two girls were expected to play together, which they did well
enough. But would they have chosen each other? Would they
have clocked each other across a church hall or playground
and edged closer with a tentative smile and the fervent hope of
making a friend?

The McCords were a noisy, effusive family, Lou and
Beattie forever bending to one of their brood, to administer
an admonition, a term of endearment, a ticking-off, a kiss or a
skelp. One moment hurtled into the next. The only person who
remained apart from the perpetual bustle was Mrs Wellsley.
Unlike Gala's Gran, Mrs Wellsley was never seen in an apron,
sleeves rolled up, chopping and peeling, scrubbing and washing
up. She wasn't seen much at all. In town she spent most of her
days at the library, in Daly's Tea Room or ensconced in her
spacious room in the McCords' house, which she referred to as
her 'suite'. Only at mealtimes did she venture into the domestic
mayhem, stiff and distant as a superior lodger. She favoured
crisply pleated skirts, blouses with lace collars, cardigans with
pearl buttons and court shoes.

On the island, Mrs Wellsley wasn't the sort to lug rugs and
toys, windbreaks, flasks and towels to the beach, to join in
the jolly caravanserai. As soon as breakfast was over she took
herself off to a quiet spot, out of harm's way, harm being unruly

brats who might splash her, deposit clumps of seaweed in her lap or, heaven forbid, attempt to bury her in sand. She settled her trim derrière into a striped deckchair, crossed her ankles and set to work on her embroidery. She was particularly fond of edifying texts:

The Path to Hell is Paved with Good Intentions
The Love of Money is the Root of All Evil
The Least Said, the Soonest Mended
Charity Begins at Home

On the island, which had a steep dark mountain at its heart, sheep trotted along the street and, in the night, invisible creatures screeched and flapped against the windowpanes. Gala shared a bedroom with Ailsa which, in an unfamiliar house, was better than sleeping alone. At first.

During the day everyone spent most of the time on the great expanse of honey-coloured sand. The children built castles, dug moats, dashed in and out of the sea, skiffed stones, poked around rockpools with nets on sticks, guddled for tiddlers. They blinked in the bright sunlight, sniffed the salty air.

Lou McCord, who was a minister in the city, would stride off across the sand, arms swinging, trousers flapping, squinting at the sky or gazing far out to sea. He'd stop suddenly, frown at a patch of sand then turn back, each time approaching his family with joy, as if he were meeting them again after a long absence. When Gala asked Ailsa why her father was always staring at nothing, Ailsa replied that he was preparing his next sermon.

Beattie was taken up with tending to baby Harris who was bald and pink, goo-gooing as he rolled around on a beach towel in a nappy and sun bonnet. When he began to girn, she put him to the breast or cradled him down to the water's edge and dipped his chipolata toes in sun-warmed shallows. At the day's end they all dripped back happily to the house, Mrs Wellsley bringing up the rear and keeping her distance. In spite of everyone removing their shoes at the door, sandy footprints trailed across the carpet.

Before tea, which the McCords called supper, the minister said Grace in his deep, treacly voice, and everybody around the table – except baby Harris who was too young to understand – and Gala, who had what Gran called a stubborn streak, shut their eyes:

For what we are about to receive...

At home, nobody said Grace at mealtimes but it wasn't saying *Thank You* for food which Gala rebelled against – and Beattie made tasty, hearty food – it was shutting her eyes to talk to God. If God was invisible, what difference did it make to close your eyes?

When the meal was over, the table cleared and the dishes washed amidst a battery of tickings off and hugs and a steady monologue from Beattie – You know I love you, dearest but you're a lazy besom and if you don't bring those plates to the sink this very minute, you can expect to feel my hand on your tender bottom – it was bathtime.

Warm, rust-coloured water slopped up and over the bathtub. Soapsuds stung eyes. Whoops and squeals competed with splashes and tears. Vigorous towelling was followed by tooth brushing. Children on tiptoes tried to see their shiny, sunburnt faces in the rusty mirror above the wash hand basin. When there was almost as much water on the bathroom lino as in the tub, it was bedtime.

Snug in flannelette pyjamas, all the peppermint-breathed children trooped back into the living room where Daddy McCord paced around, hands deep in his pockets. He made forays to the front of the room, to squint through the open window. The daylight was not yet done and the sea smell crept into the house, tickling the nostrils like a sneeze. Birds going home to roost passed the window, quick as blinks. Mrs Wellsley sat on the best armchair, not a permed curl out of place, embroidery reinstated on her pleated lap.

When she padded over to kiss Lou and Beattie goodnight, and, yes, Mrs Wellsley also inclined her cheek, a teary wobble rose in Gala's throat. This was not her own family, not her home. It was not even the McCords' home, which was down the back lane from her own house, behind a wild, wayward hedge and a slatted wooden gate with a broken handle. She was in a house on an island, away from her family for the first time in her life. Where exactly was her own home and what was happening there? Was Jas in bed already? Was Gran telling him a bedtime story? What was her family doing while she was kissing goodnight to somebody else's mummy and daddy and to a Gran who wasn't as good to kiss as her own?

The bedroom smelled of mothballs and something fishy, of hot water bottles and strangeness. Twin beds, separated by a small table and a bedside lamp, were tucked under the eaves. Stiff, mustard curtains covered the window. Dusty pink candlewick throws covered the eiderdowns. On the wall, caught in lamp's beam, hung a piece of Mrs Wellsley's handiwork: *In the Darkest Hour, I am the Light,* below a picture of Jesus.

Out of habit, Gala shut her eyes for prayers. Through thin cotton pyjama bottoms, the sandy carpet rasped against her knees, like a punishment for keeping her eyes open during Grace. Her elbows sank into puffy eiderdown, her steepled fingers rested against a crisp cool pillow.

God Bless Mummy and Daddy and Gran and Granny and Grandad Price and Jas and all the children in the world without mummies and daddies and grans and grannies and grandads and all the poor people in Africa who don't have enough food and all the sick people and the lonely people and the sad people in the world –

She opened her eyes several times, came face to face with Jesus. As Ailsa's list went on for ages, Gala tried to come up with more people to add to her own list but felt a bit of a fraud. How could praying for more people make you a better person? Wouldn't God know if you were just adding names to keep up with somebody else? If he knew then there was no point. And if he didn't know, then he couldn't really do everything he was supposed to do.

Jesus was wearing white robes, his eyes were swivelling heavenwards. His hair was long and flowing, arms outstretched but he didn't actually look open-armed and welcoming, didn't look as if he were suffering little children to come unto him. He had a faraway look. Sad and gentle, unlike her father's faraway look.

At least the Jesus in the room wasn't the terrible bleeding Jesus on the Cross that some people had on their wall, at least it wasn't the Crucifix. But Jesus on the Cross was nothing to do with the Prices or the McCords. They had the Cross and they had Jesus but not together because they weren't Catholics. They didn't have Saints either. Jesus bleeding on the Cross was for Catholics. Catholics went to schools named after Saints. And then there was Hell. Hell – what it was, where it was, why you went there and what you did or had done to you – Catholics knew all about Hell.

Grace. Prayers. Jesus. God. God might answer your prayers, wishes, requests. Never demands, you couldn't demand anything from God. He – and God was definitely a *He* – was much more likely to respond to prayers which involved helping others. You could of course pray to make yourself a better person. How to become a better person involved generosity, honesty and putting others first. Honesty was essential even though God with his superhuman powers could see into the most secret corner of your mind. He could work out whether you had bad thoughts or were telling the truth. Liars were bad. Evil. Almost as bad as trespassers and murderers.

When Ailsa finally ran out of people to pray for, the two girls climbed into the twin beds and snuggled up, still warm from the bath, damp hair steaming against cool, crisp pillows. Because of the special excitement of having someone to talk to in bed, and a burning, brimming desire to be truthful, once Gala had the blankets pulled up to her chin, she turned to Ailsa and said, without any hesitation or forethought:

I don't believe in God. Or Jesus Christ or Santa Claus.

She can't recall any verbal reply. Only Ailsa's soft eyes widening, a gap opening up, her words falling like stones between the twin beds and going on falling, into an endless gorge, a bottomless pit. Was this Hell? Were her words falling into Hell? Had her loose, seven-year-old tongue damned her so that now she, like her loose words must fall, fall and go on falling forever? The bed felt as if it were collapsing beneath her. Its cosy solidity had been a trick, an illusion. It was rotten through and through. Or she was.

The next day, the day before they went home, surely – how could she have endured any longer in the brooding climate of unease that she had created *all by herself* – nobody mentioned her pillowtalk declaration of atheism. Ailsa had told her parents, no doubt about it. Lou and Beattie knew, Gala could tell by their sharp, dark glances, what she had had the nerve, the downright God-defying insolence to come out with. And in a minister's house! There was no longer any fun to be had from jumping waves or watching her toes sink into wet sand, no pleasure in irrigation systems or sandcastle competitions. The day crawled by as if the earth had lost the will to turn.

Gala expected something to happen: a row from Beattie for trying to lead Ailsa down the road to ruin, or Lou drilling her on proofs of the existence of God but neither happened. Nothing happened. Nothing at all. Everything went quiet, extra quiet, the way a place is before a storm. But no storm came. She is sure of this. Nothing happened but something might as well have happened. Something bad. She might as well have been given no pudding or been made to sit in a corner of the room or read some terrible endless passage in the bible about *smiting* while everybody else was romping around together, one big happy family into which she'd come and poured the poison of her disbelief. She wanted to go home. So badly it hurt. To go to her own bed, pull the covers over her head and stay under them forever.

If anything eventful happened on the journey back it has been shored up beneath the silt of memory. As soon as the faithful McCords and the damnably faithless Gala Price reached the street on which both families lived, she was out of the overcrowded family saloon car and belting up the road, a logjam of *Thankyous* and *Sorrys* clogged in her throat. She rang the bell and rapped on the door until her knuckles burned.

While she'd been away, the door knob had been polished, the net of spider webs swept off the lintel. Through the letterbox, which was at eye level, she could smell soup. It was an age before the door clicked open.

Well, hello there, stranger! her father boomed. Welcome home!

There was something wrong with his grin. It was too wide and too white.

What do you think, then?

Her father wasn't a grinner. Was he really so pleased to see her?

What do you think of the teeth, my new teeth?

His new teeth were big and square and made him look like the mad, bad, comic strip dog called Gnasher. While she was doubting the existence of God on an island with a dark mountain jutting out of its heart, the dentist had extracted whatever were left of her father's real teeth, the ones with metal fillings and extensive nicotine stains, and replaced them with a gleaming set of dentures. Gala can't remember anything more about the homecoming than her father's false grin and her own damburst of tears.

Marigold Yellow

BEFORE LEAVING FOR her shift in the bar, Gala had spent the afternoon painting the living room walls marigold yellow, in an attempt to cheer up the flat. It was on the first floor of a crumbling tenement. It was miserable; everything about the flat was miserable, including the fact that, technically, she owned it. A bad move. A rush job. A take it or leave it offer-slash-ultimatum from her father. An interest-free loan – which by itself would have been a generous enough gesture – came with a condition: that she signed up for a course in teacher training. Agreeing to the conditions meant having to fit in as much bar work as she could find in order to meet the payments. Not to mention embarking on the least appealing career path she could think of.

She'd had more than her fill of teachers, at home and at school, had only been free of university for a year and her degree, her very ordinary arts degree, didn't by itself qualify her for any particular employment. And she hadn't even wanted to do the bloody degree in the first place. Seeing it through had been all about pleasing the parents, and satisfying their expectations. Up to a point. Her father just couldn't seem to help turning an Ordinary Degree into Honours when, in the pub or club, glass in one hand, cigarette in the other, he'd boast about his daughter's new status as a graduate. And still he and her mother

– who never confused Ordinary with Honours – expected her to furnish them with yet another certifiable achievement.

In the year after she graduated, she hadn't signed on the dole like plenty of her able-bodied contemporaries had done, rubbishing The System while simultaneously exploiting it, banging on about Come the Revolution, man, and skinning up another joint. She wasn't the workshy layabout her father suggested when she paid her parents a visit to ask for a loan. She'd had plenty of jobs: temporary, casual, menial, poorly paid, whatever was going. Just because she hadn't yet found something which might qualify as a respectable career option didn't mean that she wouldn't, in time.

Part of the problem was the guy she'd been living with. It had taken quite some time to work out that he liked to spend whatever money he had. Then move on to spending hers. He was no good. She'd listened to enough blues lyrics to know: he was no poor, hard-done-by guy whose woman didn't love him; he was no victim of chance who had all the cards stacked against him; no, he was a cocky bastard who got what he wanted. And if he didn't, he took it anyway, or went looking for it elsewhere.

He'd been off on the randan for several days. Something she'd said or done. Something she hadn't said or done. Nothing to do with his own aversion to looking for paid work or cleaning up while she was working, oh no. It was her fault. It was always her fault. His keys were on the table but he'd left all of his stuff, so he'd be back. He liked his stuff. And other people's.

She didn't want him back, didn't want to get drawn back into the vicious circle again, didn't want another doing, didn't want to make up. To chuck his stuff out on the landing and change the locks, she'd have liked to do that, but the strategy only worked in movies. In real life, by being denied entry, even if you've stacked everything neatly, given him a fair amount of shared possessions and attached a friendly note, wished him well in his future life, the guy is more likely to kick in the door then lay into the woman, rage cranked up to self-righteous fury.

But waiting for the inevitable wasn't easy. He was on the

hunt for another woman with a better flat and a well-paid job, who was prepared to keep him in the style to which he aspired and considered he deserved. When he found the right woman, the well-heeled, easy-going woman to replace the torn-faced bitch she'd apparently become, he'd pack up and go. It had to happen, it was for the best but she'd miss him all the same, miss what he'd once been, was already missing him.

The first floor function room was awash with green flock wallpaper and bluey-green swirly-patterned carpet. The wall lights had green plastic lampshades. It was like being inside an aquarium. A steady stream of guys stumbled in and weaved towards the bar. By the time Bert the barman had opened up the taps, the queue was three deep. Prices were higher than usual but the guys were already half tanked and didn't notice. Or care. Judging by the square clothes, square jaws, the hearty backslapping and roughhouse intimacy that comes from a childhood filled with contact sports and communal showers, the stags could cope with a few extra pence on a pint, even if they did intend to consume gallons.

Loud but well-behaved, even before the entertainment had begun, the stags were tipping lavishly. Bert maintained his dour, 'can't-be-doing-wi-the-likes-o-you-cunts' expression, served them grimly, slapped their change on the bar and pretended not to hear requests for ice, a tall glass, or a better head on the Guinness.

By the time the third round was being lined up, they were becoming impatient:

Why are we waiting! they chanted, stamping their feet and clowning around like the overgrown schoolboys they were.

Before he opened up the function room, Lally, the hotel manager, had primed Gala and Bert to get the stags to buy as much drink as possible before the entertainment arrived, but when he stuck his head in and saw that things were getting rowdy, he gave the nod.

Right! said Bert, banging on the bar for order. A wee bit housekeeping afore we start. Once the exotic dancer begins her act – her name's Cherry, by the way – that carpet is like a totally no-go zone. Picture an electric fence around it. Should the *artiste* wish to step off the Axminster and fraternise with members of the audience, that, gentlemen, is her prerogative, and hers alone. Unless yous wanna be oot the door on yer arse, keep your clogs on the parquet.

As Lally locked the door from the outside, which contravened fire regulations but prevented any stray residents from copping an unpaid-for eyeful, the stags shuffled into a tight, heavy breathing cordon around the swirly carpet. Bert dimmed the sidelights, the booming intro to Roxy Music's *Love is the Drug* flooded the fishtank function room and Cherry strode in from the Ladies' Toilets. The stags parted to let her into their midst, then closed ranks.

She was small and curvy with bouncy blonde curls and muscular calves. Her outfit was tried and tested: a clingy red dress, black fishnets, feather boa, red patent stilettos. A rope of black beads knotted at her cleavage and a red garter completed the hot stuff ensemble. The stags were already grinning like dopes.

Cherry was slick and gave a convincing impression of enjoying her work, unlike some of the sorry hopefuls Lally had auditioned the previous week, in front of a small audience composed of hotel staff. Ahead of their performance, in breathy sybillant tones, Lally had informed the girls that they need go no further than taking their tops off; there were ladies present after all. One girl had burst into tears before she'd even attempted to unclip her bra, another froze midway in her half-hearted gyrations, as if her granny had walked into the room. Perhaps it was having to do their act in the middle of the day, to a bunch of drop-jawed kitchen staff and razor-eyed barmaids, but even those who made it through until Lally switched off the music, had clearly stepped into unknown and uncomfortable territory.

Cherry was no rookie. She was giving the guys all they'd paid for and even when she was butt naked, rolling around on the seabed-effect carpet, touching herself up, flashing her fanny and doing dirty stuff with the groom's tie, she was clearly not giving away anything she hadn't given away long ago. When she wound up her act, collecting a wad of tips in the process, her sassy-arsed exit to the Ladies' was accompanied by rabid applause.

When they queued at the bar to slake their dry throats and knock back a couple more for the road, the stags were sheepish, almost apologetic, doing their best to sound sober and proper, tipping extravagantly. One guy even asked Gala for a date:

Somewhere nice, he said, with dinner. Better than this dump.

Finbar Gemmell, LLB, Solicitor, his card said. Tweed jacket, biscuit-coloured trousers, loud shirt, cropped hair in the style of a 1940s action hero. Not her type at all. Her parents would have loved him.

While Bert and Lally hustled the stags out with:

Now, gentlemen, this way please, let's be having you, we don't want to contravene our entertainments licence – Gala was sent to the toilets to give Cherry her wage.

Mind and see her off the premises, Lally added, fat palms mopping sweat from his shiny forehead.

Ta, said Cherry, counting the cash then stashing it in her already stuffed purse. Cherry's wages were a hell of a lot more than Gala made in a night of pulling pints. And how long had her act lasted – forty-five minutes?

See you around.

Cherry slipped down the service stair and out into the back lane. Nondescript, mousy haired, in a plain dark coat and decidedly unkinky boots, Cherry might have been one of the housekeeping staff, it not for the blonde wig poking out of her kitbag and the self-satisfied smile that comes from having cleaned up.

Once the glasses had been washed, the till checked and the functions of the function room over and done with, Bert, who wasn't known for his generosity or social skills, suggested a late drink. Bert wasn't Gala's ideal drinking companion but nor was she in a rush to get home.

They were on their third for the road, in a dreggy pub where Bert was on first-name terms with the management. It was the type of place that had only recently opened its doors to women: no juke box, no TV, no fruit machine, just grimy wainscotting, the thick fug of smoke, the dull gleam of optics and the low grumble of grizzled old guys putting the world to rights.

The way you handled that crowd tonight, Bert said for the third time, I was really impressed.

Piece of cake.

Scum, said Bert. Rich scum.

Well-behaved scum. Generous scum.

Guilt money, said Bert. Think they can toss a few coins our way and everything's hunky dory. The shame. You shouldn't have to see that kind of thing, you really shouldn't. Disgusting, so it is.

Lally paid me a better rate than usual, said Gala. And I need the money.

You're an attractive woman, a very attractive woman, d'you ken what I'm saying?

Tell that to the guy I've been living with.

Any guy who's lucky enough to have you as a girlfriend must be on cloud nine.

I've gotta get going, Bert. College tomorrow.

College? College? Good looks plus brains – a winning combination! A jackpot. A bleeding jackpot. Good looks plus a jackpot –

Gala body-swerved Bert's goodnight lunge and set off briskly, feigning sobriety and giving other late-night carousers a wide berth. At the foot of the Walk, in the middle of the road, a couple were screaming the odds at each other. She kept walking. The last time she'd attempted to intercede in a domestic, both parties had turned on her and redirected their aggression.

There was a depressing smell of cat piss in the closemouth and a pile of rubbish the wind had blown in. She took the stairs slowly. They needed to be cleaned. Again. It was her turn. Again. The door to her flat was hanging on its hinges, the wood split around the frame. Had she been burgled?

Hello, she said. Hello? Her words were thin and papery, barely escaping her mouth.

The hall light was bleak. The hall was bleak. Coming back to a battered-in door was bleak. She paused, half expecting some marauder to appear but after a while it was clear that whoever had broken in had been and gone. In the hall, a photo lay on the floor under the smashed glass of the clip frame. Of the two of them, in the early days, when they couldn't get enough of each other, when she could do no wrong.

In the kitchen, the kettle was missing. And the coffee pot. In the bedroom, the wardrobe gaped. The cowboy boots he'd splashed out on rather than paying his share of the bills were gone. The leather jacket and most of his clothes. The record player was also gone. Must have taken a taxi. Or got somebody with a car to help him out. Quite a few of her LPs. The best ones, of course. The rejects were strewn across the bed. So, not a burglar. As such. In the living room, across the freshly painted marigold wall, scrawled with what looked like tomato ketchup: SPLITTING.

Wood

MAHOGANY. CHERRY. TEAK. Walnut. Oak. Box. Ebony. Gouge. Mallet. Chisel. Veiner. Fluter. Spoon. Fishtail. Hard wood. Soft wood. When her father was working with wood, the studio smelled tangy and sweet. Resin oozed like syrup from knots and the floor was strewn with curly gold-brown shavings which blew around like autumn leaves. The work in progress was clutched between the jaws of a vice. The clock of hammer on chisel was deep and regular and what began as a dull block of wood became, chip by chip, a mass of chiselled waves and then, slowly, slowly, a back and a belly began to appear, then a head, a leg, a fluffy tail.

The squirrel was a commission. In the Price household, the word commission had currency, particularly when Gala's father wanted to get out to his studio and Vera wanted him to fix some household appliance, oversee the children's homework or give Jas a bath.

I don't have time. I've got a *commission* to finish.

The word had weight, value. A specific value and an unspecific one. Cash and kudos. It brought a glint to his eye. Somebody had asked him to make something to order, had promised him some money for his work. It brought a glint but it also brought pacing and smoking and misgivings about whether Lady Sprules of Piggott Hill, Field Marshall Barger

Dockett, Miss Rowardennan of Bildean or Reverend Dunston of Carstairs – the names of those who'd commissioned work wound around the house like isobars intimating fair weather or foul – would like what they got and pay up, on time or at all.

The commissioned red squirrel, which began life as a hunk of reddish wood, took its reference points from a real, grey squirrel. The smaller, more delicate red squirrels were rare. The grey had almost wiped them out. For half a year a grey squirrel ate, slept and flung itself around the wire mesh cage her father built on to the back of the garage, which he had turned into another studio. The car, a new-to-them, roomier vehicle, sat out on the driveway under a fibreglass carport which only protected it from rain, snow or hail if there was no accompanying wind, which was also rare.

Not long back the Price family had moved house, moved out of town, away from the dinky terrace houses with Scandinavian-style gables and suitably named streets: Norse Road, Danes Drive, to a new build in a new development – a detached house with rows of half-built lookalikes encroaching on what had been open farmland. When it rained, the newly tarmacadamed streets ran white with cement dust.

The area was popular with expanding families, keen to get out of town. It was lighter, brighter than what they'd left behind. Roughcast exteriors were whitewashed, lawns were tender and dotted with baby shrubs and saplings. Her father put in a woven wooden fence along one side of their garden. On the other, the neighbours had planted a hedge. Privet for privacy. No less than a detached house deserved.

In one of the half-built houses across the road, Gala had found the squirrel. She had been fooling around with some of the neighbourhood boys, leaping out of unglazed windows, holding aloft umbrella parachutes, landing on bags of sand and cement, balancing on open struts which would, in time, support a floor or ceiling. Safety provision was casual, to say the least. Was there even a *Danger – Keep Out!* sign?

That day she had something else in mind: to scale the unfinished roof which was covered with some kind of bitumen underlay. So far, none of the gang had attempted the feat. After the others had gone home for their meal, she was weighing up possible routes when she was distracted by an insistent squealing. The source was a pile of masonry. Up close she saw a bristling snout, and sharp, bright teeth which could well have belonged to a rat, but rats had thin, bald tails and the tail she saw was the fat, furry question mark of a squirrel. The poor thing was trapped between concrete blocks too heavy for her to shift.

The animal continued to squeal as she ran home to fetch help. It must have been a spring evening. There's a smell of gorse in the memory, sweet as coconut.

A squirrel? said her father. Now there's a spot of luck.

Protected by a pair of heavy-duty gardening gloves, he managed to extricate the animal but, rather than setting it free, her father, muttering the words *commission* and *perfect,* slipped it into the shoebox he'd brought along for the purpose and, with a look of immense satisfaction, carried it home. The squirrel scrabbled desperately.

He kept the squirrel in a wooden crate while he constructed a run by attaching chickenwire to the back wall of the garage. The enclosure was spacious, with height as well as depth. It contained a 'climbing feature', a couple of flexible boughs, a fence post perch, a water hole made from a car tyre and a straw-lined bread bin to provide shelter from the elements.

The squirrel was male and must have been a young thing which didn't know any better because after a few days of throwing itself against the mesh, it appeared to settle into life in captivity. Jas named it Frisky and was forever wanting to handle it and feed it. It was, unsurprisingly, fond of nuts, but also had a sweet tooth and liked nothing better than an oblong of Fry's Turkish Delight. In the right mood, Frisky would nibble cutely. In the wrong mood he would bite the hand that fed him.

Gala's father made numerous sketches. Some he did from outside the enclosure but for close-ups he bought the smallest dog collar he could find – intended for one of the popular miniature breeds – Chihuahua or Pekinese – and rigged up a high perch. He tried to bribe the squirrel with chocolate to sit on the perch – to sit still! – so he could take some photographs without interlocking diamonds of chickenwire spoiling his view and putting his subject out of focus. He received several nasty bites, and put both the squirrel and himself in a bad mood for days.

At first, neighbourhood kids were keen to stick fingers, noses and tongues through the mesh, to toss in peanuts and chunks of chocolate. But there was limited fun in an animal you couldn't hold without wearing heavy-duty gardening gloves, and interest turned to boredom and disapproval: it was a wild animal, and a wild animal shouldn't be kept in a cage, not even an artistic, spacious, airy cage.

Once the commission was done, once the chisel marks had been sanded off the reddish wood, the surface buffed and polished and the patron of the arts had paid up, Gala's father set Frisky free. She was glad to see him bound off down the garden, across the street and off towards the fields and woodland which lay beyond the new builds. Though she hoped he might return for a nibble of Turkish delight, he never did. As the reddish wood suggested a red squirrel but the sculpture was modelled on one of the bulkier, grey variety, the end result was something of a hybrid; its recipient wasn't entirely satisfied with the result.

Was the summer of the squirrel the same season her father had a large rock dumped by a forklift truck in the middle of the lawn? A centrepiece, he called it. A focal point. Was that when he built the stone-walled swimming pool too small to swim in and which soon became rife with insects and algae? And when did he decide to further break up the monotony of the new lawn with a pathway in the voguish, smashed-up slab effect called crazy paving? The rock became a local joke, the pool a pointless, festering trough. The crazy paving lived up to its name.

Dog Obedience

BY THE TIME the dog arrived, the Price family had once again flitted, out of a new house and into an old, decrepit one which provided Miles with many years' worth of renovating projects: putting in dormer windows, building upstairs bedrooms for the children, moving doors, knocking down walls and, to everyone's eventual regret, constructing a dinette (imitation wood, imitation leather) in what had formerly been a pantry.

The place came with a spacious, unkempt garden back and front. Through the front ran a burn narrow enough to leap across but wide enough for the leap to be a challenge. The grass was knee-high and home to throngs of frogs. In its wild state the garden was a big draw for local kids, providing ideal terrain for crawling around, commando-style, on your belly.

The grass didn't stay tall for long. At the end of the summer it was scythed, mowed, the Sleeping Beauty tangle of briars which had once been rosebeds was dug up and turfed over, the borders cleared of undergrowth and new shrubs planted in neat rows. The grass restored to a respectable short back and sides, neighbourhood kids drifted away and the garden and its reclaimed herbaceous border all too soon brought Gala an additional chore: weeding. And then came the dog.

She can't remember wanting a dog, didn't like dogs much, the barking and biting, the drooling, the pong. Perhaps Jas had been keen. He was more the animal lover. He had a guinea pig called Bumble, a low-slung furry sausage on daft wee legs, with bee stripes and a shrill, relentless squeak. Rather than doing anything useful like collecting pollen and turning it into honey, Bumble bumbled around haphazardly and in typical rodent style, gnawed. Anything. Everything. But preferably plastic, and whatever it coated.

One evening, the assembled Prices were squished together on the couch, watching *Steptoe and Son*. Yet again, Harold Steptoe's chances of a click had been scuppered by his grubby, sneaky old dad. Harold was working up to the kind of self-righteous lather which would lead to him spitting out the catchphrase: *You dirty old man!* when there was a classic blue flash, an outbreak of mini-explosions inside the TV, like corn popping from its kernels. No programmes for a week. Bumble had gnawed through the wires.

When the dog arrived, a wild-eyed squitter of nervous energy, Bumble scuttled fatly into his cage, preferring to take exercise on a rattling wheel than take a chance on survival on the living room floor. The dog didn't just throw himself about and bark incessantly, he got everyone else chasing after him and yelling. At him. At each other. There were times, and not all to do with the dog, when Gala wished she had a similar bolt-hole to the guinea pig.

Bongo was a fox terrier with a wiry, corkscrew coat, a bearded block of a head and a stiff, permanently vibrating tail. Her father's choice. Gala wouldn't have gone for a jittery little yapper. If she had to have a dog, she'd have opted for a loping, languid variety, with soulful eyes and a silky coat. Bongo moved like overwound clockwork. Even in sleep he quivered, primed to spring and yap as soon as he woke. *Down, Bongo, down!*

Initially Miles was proud of his choice.

Pedigree, he said. Good breeding.

You'll have to walk him yourself, said Vera.

Had he been offered the dog in part payment for a commission from one of the wealthy folk who lived deep in the country on acres of their own land because they were, unfortunately, a bit strapped for cash? Or was the dog an extra, casually thrown in with payment, like a tip? – *The bitch has littered, so here you are, Miles. Take him away with you. Give him a good home. Think nothing of it.*

Perhaps he'd just run into someone who was trying to offload some unwanted pups and been led to believe he'd got himself a bargain. Whatever Bongo cost, he was no bargain.

As well as buying a collar, a leash and a dog whistle, her father bought himself a tweed hat with a grouse feather in the band, and a waxed jacket. Before venturing on to the street for walkies, he attempted to drum some basic training into Bongo's frazzled synapses. The training sessions were a trial to all concerned. The dog couldn't or wouldn't obey a simple order. Miles persevered, repeated the orders, louder each time and redder in the face. Any success he had could only be attributable to luck.

On the order to *Sit!* Bongo threw himself at his master's ankle. When called upon to *Stay!* he sprung in the air, tail ticking like a metronome. When a ball was thrown for him to *Fetch!* he flattened himself against the grass. *Heel!* had the worst effect. Instead of trotting obediently behind her father as he marched across the grass, the dog began to chase his tail. And once Bongo caught sight of that silly little docked stump, he whirled in tighter, dog-dervish circles until, dizzy and deranged, he puked on the re-constituted lawn.

Highly strung, said her father, hoarse and purple in the face.

Inbred, said her mother.

I'll get a mop, said Gran.

Leave it, said her father. Gala can do it.

Why can't Jas do it? Gala whined.

I'm too young, said Jas.

Yes, he's too young, said her father. He'd make a mess of it.

After the initial training period was declared over and in spite of the fact that the dog was clearly unable to comprehend or respond to simple instructions, or was temperamentally disinclined to do so, Miles began taking Bongo for walks. Very short walks, barely to the end of the street and back, and involving very little actual walking, the main purpose being to let him lift his leg and do his business somewhere other than the garden.

As soon as he tried to attach the leash to the collar, Bongo bit him. As for walking beside his master in an orderly, well-bred fashion, the dog yanked so hard on the lead, he nearly choked. His tongue swelled. His breath departed his slavering chops in long, ragged gasps. When he lost interest in straining at the leash, he ran rings round Miles's legs, entwining them both in a tense, irascible bond. *Down, Bongo, down! For Christ's sake do what you're bloody told.* Nothing he shouted at Bongo worked. But he didn't give up shouting. He could be heard the length of the street.

The desire for canine obedience might have been the main reason for getting a dog but Bongo's lack of obedience became one of Miles's most visible failures. Normal, affectionate patting set off tail-chasing or ankle-snapping. Bongo was incapable of fetching anything other than bits of dead birds that cats had left lying around. As for obedience, Miles's hopes of having a living creature around which would willingly fawn and do his master's bidding came to nothing. What he got, what all the Price family got, was a fractious, serial vomiter.

The dog didn't restrict his vomiting to his own garden but boisterously leaped the baby hedge and performed his party piece on the neighbours' lovingly tended lawn. Gala was expected to clean that up as well. When Bongo was given away to an unsuspecting farmer, she wasn't unbearably sad about his departure: sluicing dog vomit ceased to be one of her chores.

Living with Marlene

WHEN EXACTLY DID Marlene take up residence, she of the husky croon and sculpted cheekbones, pencilled brows and irises which slid up under heavy lids like a china doll laid on its back?

Gran said she looked *sent*, whatever that meant. How long had she been lurking in a corner of some shadowy celluloid lounge bar, like a glittering, fishnet-stockinged spider, lying in wait for Gala's father, willing him and countless other men of his generation to succumb to entanglement in her web?

Vera moaned about the volume at which Miles played his music and insisted that it distracted her piano pupils. She complained about the volume of most things but especially her husband's taste in music and especially his long-playing record of Marlene Dietrich. In the early days, Maria Callas or Victoria de los Ángeles would be given a spin on the turntable but at some point he began to leave the other songbirds in their dusty cardboard sleeves. When was it that he only had ears for Marlene?

Was Vera jealous of Marlene? Is the question worth asking? Though Gala's mother had in her youth been good-looking, if more in a brisk, no-nonsense Katherine Hepburn way than in the sultry manner of Marlene, by her late thirties her appearance was unremarkable. She had good enough bone structure, her hair was still a luxuriant auburn but she had thickened around the middle and lost what little interest she'd ever had in fashion.

No match for a blonde German bombshell who displayed her assets with slit skirts and plunging necklines.

The fact that Marlene was German didn't quite add up. Though by the time Gala was born the war had been over for a decade, the Germans were still perceived as enemies. As were the Italians. Hitler and Mussolini – everybody knew they were baddies. And the Nazis, the Gestapo, the ss, the Blackshirts and the Brown. There were plenty British or American war films around to remind you whose side you were on. The Prices were on the side which spoke English properly – or, under exceptional conditions, in an American accent. The French Resistance, who wore berets and smoked non-stop, were foolhardy daredevils, sometimes heroic. But anybody who spoke English in a German accent, even if it was a patently fake German accent, was undoubtedly a baddy. In playground war games, those assigned to be Gerries could never emerge as deserving winners.

Vera certainly didn't have a deep, drawly, heavily accented singing voice. She could keep a tune but there was nothing sensual or seductive about her voice. And even if there had been, she certainly wouldn't have wasted it on trashy popular songs. For her, it was classical music or nothing. She would be lahlahing and dahdahing along to Beethoven, Mozart or Chopin in the living room while, through the wall in the studio, Miles would hum along with Marlene, 'Falling in Love Again' would crackle and scrape as he confronted his work in progress:

dah dah de *dah* dah *like moths around a flame*

dah dah de *dah* dah, *I know I'm not to blame*

If Marlene wasn't to blame for Gala's father retreating at every available opportunity to whatever extension to whatever house was designated *the studio,* with the whisky and the fags, to commune with a lilting accordion and weeping strings, with raunchy trumpets and soldiers loitering outside barracks in the rain, and truckloads of smouldering desire, who was?

While Gran baked buns for supper or chopped onions and grated carrots for tomorrow's soup and Vera wandered around the house counting out five-finger exercises as some piano pupil plinked away in the front room, while Jas raced his Dinky cars along the carpet, while Gala, due to some complex yearning to connect with her father, harboured romantic fantasies about following in his artistic footsteps, and drew ponies and glamour girls (once she'd finished her homework, of course), her father wallowed in his own fantasies:

He would have a full head of hair, a double-breasted suit with knife-edge lapels, a glass of fine malt in one hand, a cigarette, or possibly a cheroot, in the other. Across a swanky lounge bar, a solitary Marlene would puff a smoke ring into the fuggy air. With nothing more than a slow bat of her eyelashes, she'd invite him to join her. Or, if hot jazz were trumpeting through the smoky room, she might just sashay across the floor on the shapeliest and most highly insured legs this side of the Equator. And shimmy him into oblivion.

Of course Marlene wasn't just a good-time girl; she didn't shy from the dark, bitter side of things. She had even recorded a song about a hanging: *If he swings from the string he will hear the bell ring, and then there's an end to poor Tommy* – Gala could picture her father committing a crime on behalf of Marlene: a daring, heroic crime of passion, a wrong righted, just vengeance meted out. She could picture him standing, forlorn but stoic, a noose around his neck, while the blonde bombshell blew him a farewell kiss. She could picture it but what did it mean? Why would her father *want to buy some illusions, slightly used, almost new?*

Of course Miles wasn't just wallowing in romantic sentiment and anybody who had the nerve to think that didn't know the first thing about the artistic temperament. He was working, working! And perish the thought that anybody might forget it. If Gala was sent to the studio with yet another mug of coffee, he might acknowledge receipt of the hot beverage, he might not. He might simply pause in what he was doing and turn the record over. Everybody in the house knew the lyrics by heart. Her voice slipped under the doors, along the passageways and through the walls, the black velvet voice of Marlene who had stolen Gala's father.

Amateur Dramatics

GALA HADN'T REGISTERED the changes in her father's facial grooming until the photos arrived, monochrome headshots which portrayed a sneering, or leering, mutton-chopped, Victorian villain. As he brandished them at the family, loosely assembled in the living room, she realised that he now sported whiskers which ran the length of his jaw, leaving only a small clean-shaven wedge of chin. His moustache was no longer of the toothbrush variety but extended beyond his mouth and had been waxed into points at the tips, stiff as old paintbrushes.

Well, do I look the part?

What part?

The leading role. Lots of dramatic action. And a bit of love interest thrown in!

At the mention of love interest, her mother sniffed, folded her arms. Her father, in a gaudy shirt and a paisley cravat paced around the living room, muttering the phrase *muffins for tea* repeatedly.

Well, what do you think?

What are muffins? Jas asked.

Teacakes, said Gran.

Are we having muffins for tea?

We've awready had tea.

Are they nice? Will I like them?

Naethin like a hot, buttered muffin, dearie. I'll mak ye some one day.

Tomorrow?

Soon. That's a promise.

So what do you think, Lottie? Do I look like a Victorian villain? Closer to your era than mine.

Gran obediently studied each of the nasty photos in turn, pronounced them *very good quality* then took herself off to the kitchen to make herself useful. Vera cast her eye over them, said she hoped he wasn't intending to put them up in the sitting room as they'd give her pupils nightmares, and exited in the direction of whoever was stumbling over *Für Elise*.

The curtain rises upon the rather terrifying darkness of late afternoon – the zero hour, as it were, before the feeble dawn of gas light and tea, Miles projected into the living room. It's the stage directions, he added. To set the scene.

Jas goggled at the photos then dashed off in search of his guinea pig.

Why do you want to look nasty? Gala asked.

Publicity! he replied. Publicity! For the local rag. I'll be the one to bring in the crowds, even if one of the leading ladies – my stage *wife* – thinks the whole show revolves around her. I may not have her years of experience, and they're beginning to show, I can tell you, but I have what it takes. Talent! Presence! My stage *wife* has been treading the boards for God knows how long but in terms of talent, or presence, you'd be hard put to notice it.

A somnambulist, Bella. Have you ever seen such a person? … that funny glazed, dazed look of the wandering mind – that body that acts without the soul to guide it? Then again my stage maid, now she has talent, presence, and promise. *We ought to keep up some pretences, you know.*

Her father tried to replicate a few of the photographic grimaces.

Is promise the same as talent? Gala asked.

Close, he said. Close.

Gala hauled herself along the mock leather bench-seat in the dinette, concentrated on her spelling for the following day:

wishful
wilful
skilful
hopeful
thankful
grateful

You know, Bella, that must be a very superb sensation. To lose yourself entirely in the character of someone else. I flatter myself I could have made an actor.

He paced around, repeating his lines with different emphasis. Gala opened her jotter and wrote:

     wishful

wishful
  wishful

Jas tried to coax the guinea pig out from under the sofa.

What d'you think? Do I sound convincingly villainous? Look at me when I'm talking to you. Do I sound like a villain?

Jas nodded solemnly then resumed crawling around the sofa.

What about you, Gala? Would you be scared? Would I strike the fear of death into you?

She also nodded, hesitantly.

Well, he said, I can see nobody in this house fully appreciates my dramatic talent.

He picked up his jacket, stuck his pipe in his mouth – the pipe was another recent affectation – and went off to rehearsals, leaving his headshots spread over the sideboard. As he went out of the back door, at the front door Vera trilled *Bye-bye* to one pupil and ushered in another.

Gala picked up the photos, making sure not add tell-tale fingerprints, and carefully turned them face down. If anybody were to ask why she had done this, her answer was prepared: to protect them from damage.

The date for the performance had been set, rehearsals had begun in earnest, her father had committed himself and couldn't let the show down. He saw things through, he claimed. Wasn't a quitter. And in spite of his many complaints about the cast – *If I have to listen to that imbecile hamming it up one more time! The leading lady fluffed her lines and held everybody up! The nit-wit who plays the detective is too big for his boots. My stage maid tried to steal my thunder!* – he came home from rehearsals in fine fettle, flushed in the face and more than usually expansive.

The idea of seeing her father treading the boards was all very well, but the idea of him playing a baddy and striding around in a menacing manner was another matter. To play the part of a villain, didn't you have to have some villainy in you, waiting to show its face?

The night arrived, wet and windy. Due to some last-minute preparations, the audience had to queue outside the church hall, which was tucked away down a muddy, overgrown path, close to the railway line. Bushes swished and dripped and gave off a smell of rot. The streetlamps were smothered with dead moths. A poster of Miles, snarling, was tacked to the door of the hall; it flapped in the wind.

Gran was dressed in her best wool coat and felt hat. Jas was wearing a check shirt and bow-tie beneath his anorak. He snuggled up against Gran for warmth. Vera, who had pinned up her hair more tidily than usual, wore Coral Pink lipstick and the flamingo coat, as Miles insisted on calling it, though it was a flame orange and weren't flamingos a deep sugary pink? Her father was colour blind. *Partially,* he insisted. A very slight colour defect. Nothing to make a song and dance about. Red/ Green. Common or garden. But his partial colour blindness, to his everlasting regret, was enough of a physiological defect to keep him out of the RAF during the war.

Vera's coat, behind which Gala stood, half-hidden, was

long and flared and out of date. The other women in the queue
– apart from the grannies in felt hats and wool coats which
smelled like wet sheep – wore short, straight coats and tight-
fitting skirts. Their hair was bobbed or back-combed and sat
stiffly on their shoulders. They were restless and talkative.

Looks like a bad lot, that Mr Manningham.

You're telling me. Wouldn't want to meet him on a dark
night!

Oh, I don't know. Maybe he's a loveable rogue.

Loveable rogues love you and leave you.

But it's fun while it lasts!

Shrieks, giggles, sparring brollies, high-heeled boots splashing
in puddles. Vera's face had a blank, turned-to-stone look. If
she knew anybody in the queue, it was patently obvious that
she had no intention of acknowledging the fact. Gran smiled
indiscriminately and patted Jas's damp curls.

Eventually the door was opened by a small man with
bristling eyebrows, a purple velvet jacket and a yellow bow tie.

Apologies, apologies. A technical hitch, my good people.
But all's well that ends well and the show must go on!

The crowd bundled in. Vera led the way to an empty row
of seats near the back and positioned herself next to the wall,
pressed her back against the chair and stuck her chin up so high
that all she could have seen was the rafters.

Whit a treat, said Gran, smiling in all directions. It's no
a'body gets to see their daddy in a play!

Where is he? said Jas.

He'll be waiting in the wings, dear. That's whit they dae
afore the show starts.

Wings?

That's jist whit they ca' bits o the stage ye canny see.

Is he going to fly?

I didny hear him say owt aboot flyin.

Peter Pan flew onto the stage.

So he did. Whit a grand memory ye've got! And you just a
wee tot when we went to see *Peter Pan*. I dinny think *Gaslight*
is that kind o a play, mind. I dinny think there's ony flyin. But

here, see whit I've found!

She held out a bag of fruit gums.

Share them wi yir sister, there's a good boy.

Around them the audience scraped into their seats, shuffled and clunked and clattered until the lights went down and the curtains creaked open.

The set was a gloomy sitting room with heavy furniture, a fireplace and, on the table, a gas lamp with a fringed shade. Miles was standing by the curtains, heavily made up, looking every inch a bad'un even before he'd said or done a thing. A haggard woman was slumped in an armchair with a doomed look on her face.

Gala sat through the performance, arms pressed tightly across her ribs, belly tight and sore, her face hot, mouth dry, willing it all to be over. As soon as possible. It wasn't at all how she wanted to see her father behave, even if it was only pretend. Underneath the silly whiskers and the painted, frowning brows, it was still her father.

From the first *What are you doing, Bella?* Mr Manningham was bad through and through, a man who'd stop at nothing to torment his wife: he tried to make her think she was going mad by hiding things and accusing her of losing them; he promised to take her out for a treat, to the theatre, then cancelled just out of devilment; he humiliated her in front of the servants and flirted brazenly with the tarty maid.

There was no end to his nastiness. His wife was well on the way to becoming a nervous wreck. He threatened her with the madhouse. One day, when he said he was going out but was actually up in the attic, searching for jewels which belonged to another woman he had murdered years ago, in the same house, the gaslight dipped and Mrs Manningham knew it was her husband because she'd noticed the lights dipping before and she wasn't stupid, or mad and in fact wasn't his wife because he was still married to somebody else but she was very frightened. She was right to be frightened because he was dangerous, a murderer who might have murdered again if the detective who was pretty stupid but at least on her side, had not helped to save Mrs Manningham from her fate. And then, because she was not really his wife, she could testify, she could get her revenge; she could see him swing.

The curtains closed raggedly and when Miles came out to take a bow, the audience booed. Delighted by the response, he bowed again and made his nastiest face. The curtains flopped back to reveal the rest of the cast and the audience whooped. In all, there were five curtain calls and a storm of applause. When the house lights went up, Vera was the first to button up her coat. The flame orange clashed with the blazing crimson of her cheeks.

4x, Hut b and the End of a Possible Career

FRIDAY AFTERNOON. EARLY June. 4x were trudging up the steps of the portacabin classroom otherwise known as Hut b, yawning, groaning with intent, humphing and galumphing, butting and shoving each other against desks they'd outgrown mentally as well as physically, swinging schoolbags from shoulders, elbows, necks, teeth. 4x's schoolbags rarely contained any books and the only reason the students showed up at school at all was because they were legally obliged to do so. Most would leave in a month. Those who hadn't turned sixteen by the summer break would leave by Christmas.

The country lads were broad, brawny, laconic, the country lasses solid and silent and old before their time: out of uniform some could have been mistaken for middle-aged wifies. The town boys were spotty and skinny, the girls quick and sharp-tongued and heavily made up. The country kids were going back to the family farm, to something with the forestry or the Hydro-Electric Board, to the ingrained cynicism of Highland hotel kitchens. Career options for the town kids: supermarket checkout operator, van driver, barmaid, shop assistant, mechanic, distillery worker. From what they told Gala, they weren't too fussed what they did for a job as long the wage packet arrived on time. And for town or country lads whose horizons extended beyond their birthplace, there were always the rigs.

The word in the staffroom was that there was little point, or let's be honest, no point at all, in trying to actually teach 4x anything. Too thick, too thrawn, too stubborn, too lazy, too sexed up, too doped up to justify any effort on the part of the teaching staff. Keep the buggers as docile as possible. Occupy them with the mindless completion of multiple choice worksheets, prevent them from vandalising the classrooms, pass the time somehow, anyhow. Don't, whatever you do, expect, or worse, encourage them to think. If they give you cheek, belt them. If they throw their weight around, belt them. If you can't administer a stiff enough lash with the two-pronged Lochgelly, send them to the head who will, in accordance with his responsibility payments and years of experience, do the job for you.

Not that being belted on a regular basis bothered 4x unduly. They were tough, they could take it. A smarting palm was a small price to pay for winding up a dominie with bare-faced cheek, dumb insolence or downright loutishness. Gala didn't subscribe to such a barbaric, outdated approach to class control. Studying the previous year for her certificate in secondary English teaching, she had read Ivan Illich's *Celebration of Awareness* and Piaget's *Play, Dreams and Imitation in Children*, Bruno Bettelheim's *The Uses of Enchantment* and A.S. Neill's writings on Summerhill, self-governance and pupil power. Instead of attempting to knock sense into the young people, she wanted to be their friend. Refusing to believe that 4x was incapable of learning anything, she brought in Dylan's protest songs, traditional ballads which championed the underdog, underground magazines, chapbooks of Russian, Vietnamese and Chilean poetry. Vernacular poetry, poetry which incorporated swearwords and references to sex and drugs, poetry as rock 'n' roll.

Putting aside the inherited departmental worksheets, she tried and tried to draw 4x out of their defensive skins and value their own experience and opinions. They didn't want to be drawn out.

Why wid ye want tae ken that, Miss?

Whit're ye gonny dae wi ma opinion?

How's this gonny be ony use tae me?

They dug in their heels, acted thick so she'd back off, leave them in peace, give up trying to free their inner selves, to express – *Ye must be jokin, Miss!* – their feelings.

The hut was baking. The windows wouldn't open and the classroom smelled of chalk dust, farts and other assorted odours of adolescence. It was the first fine day in weeks. The grassy bank beyond the huts was lush and speckled with daisies, buttercups, clover.

Don't sit down yet, she said, not that anybody was near the point of doing so. We're going to take our work outside. Fresh air and sunshine will do us all good. Cheering was followed by suspicion.

Are ye allowed, Miss?

I don't see why not. You're not going to have a carry-on, are you?

We're 4X, Miss. We aye cairry on.

We're famous for it. The famous 4X.

Cairry on 4X!

There's nae desks, so we canna write.

Ye canna write onyway, man. Ye're illiterate.

And you're a fuckin psycho.

We're going to read a play.

Aw naw!

By Shakespeare. If you prefer, we can stay inside and write job application letters.

A play, a play!

Okay. So when we leave the building, and after we leave it, you must keep the noise to a minimum. What do I mean by a minimum?

Dinna ken, Miss.

Who knows what a minimum is?

It's in music. A crotchet and a minimum.

A crotch and a mini Mum! Dirty bastard!

Has it tae dae wi a Mini? A Mini's the weeest car. And the weeest skirt. So a Mini Mum must be the weeest Mum.

Close. In a way. A minimum is the smallest amount of something.

See, ah wis richt.

A Mini's no the weeest car. A Bubble Car's the weeest.

That's no a car, man, that's a joke.

Keeping the noise to a minimum *means* – as I know you know – keep it down. We don't want to disturb Mr Forbes next door.

Ah dae. He's a snidey bam. Asked ma sister if she wis related tae ony Cro-Magnons.

Could his geography class no cam oot tae? Some crackin talent in 2B.

Aye. Aw they soft contours and jaggedy peaks.

Ravines.

Crevices, man. Tak a dekko at the crevices on wee Corrie Ardnamurchan.

That's enough, Gordie.

Aye, shut it Gordie.

Scrubland.

Like Effie Phelan?

If I can't trust you to behave, we stay indoors.

We're just thinking aboot Geography, Miss. Thickets! Gullies! Ravines!

This is your last warning –

Aye, shut yir dirty gob, Gordie.

Didna ken ah kent aw that aboot geography, man.

The class spread out in a loose circle on the sloping bank. Some of the girls took the opportunity to let their short skirts ride up even further, exposing great expanses of pallid thigh. Boys rolled up shirt sleeves and loosened ties. Why hadn't Gala thought of this before? Sunshine, fragrant air. The kids were loosening up, becoming gentler with each other, and with themselves. They nuzzled, tickled, stuck buttercups under chins, picked daisies, gazed past the confines of the school grounds towards the jagged peaks of the bens and blue, summer sky.

See yon plane, that's on its way tae London.

How d'ye ken that?

It's only the London planes fly that particular route. D'ye no ken onythin?

They chewed stalks of grass and sprawled, eyes closed, pretending to fall asleep.

Can we dae this every Friday, Miss?

Okay, everybody. You've all heard of William Shakespeare?

Auld Willie, aye. Why does a'body go on aboot him? He's been dead for whit, three hunner years?

A bit more.

A three-hunner-year-auld Willie, man! It wid be like a wee, shrivelled-up dog turd.

But whit aboot a three-hunner-year-auld malt? That wid be somethin!

That wid buy ye a castle.

Buy ye Loch Ness.

The haill o the Western Isles, man, and ye'd still hae change for Orkney and Shetland.

If some bugger hadna bought them awready.

They've no been sold, have they?

No yet, but there's folk hae a mind tae it. And if they've a mind tae it and the dosh tae back them up, whit's tae stop them?

Ye canna sell aff the islands. Where wid the Wee Frees gae for starters?

They'd aw come ower tae the mainland and wreak havoc wi the relaxed drinkin laws. And then they'd move on tae fornication- that's shaggin by the way, girls – so yous wid aw be in big, big trouble.

Shakespeare, said Gala. The play which, by the way, is a 5A text.

Whoa, Miss. We're the dumdums.

The dregs.

The dross.

The eejits.

Aye but ah'll bet maist o 5A couldna strip doon a tractor, or birth a lamb.

5A *dinna need* tae strip doon tractors or birth lambs. They *dinna want* tae be crofters. And

4X *dinna want* tae ken aboot Willie Shakespeare.

Sit up, now. Everybody. The play is a love story about two young people divided by family feuds.

Ach weel, that happens. Ma sister's winchin Jeemie MacLeod and ma auld man willna speak tae a MacLeod. If he caught ma sister wi Jeemie he'd leather her. And whit he'd dae tae Jeemie! An aw ower some shite that went doon way back afore the boy wis born. Forgive and forget, I say, but the auld man canna. Or willna.

Yon's the biggest loada shite. Folk no lettin bygones be bygones. Raking up the muck o the past.

Aye, it's nae your fault yir mammy's a slag.

Fuck you. Ye dinna even ken yir faither.

The discussion moved from parental shortcomings, politics, the church, to the social stigma of being 4X, to the state of the town, the country, the world. Gala was so caught up in listening to 4X talking about stuff which meant something to them that she didn't notice the head of department, Jockie Kilgore, striding towards her, gown flapping, or the bevy of visitors in his wake.

Good afternoon, class. 4X, is it? And what, Miss Price, is your explanation for this *al fresco* lesson? Is the classroom on fire? Has there been a flood? A plague of locusts?

Good afternoon, Mr Kilgore. The hut was too hot because the windows don't open and I thought –

Too hot? We're not in Aden, Miss Price. We're not on the burning sands of the Sahara where the heat can take the skin off your feet! We're in *the Scottish Highlands*. A *temperate* climate.

4X had become eerily quiet.

And what, may I ask, is the content of this lesson you took it upon yourself to conduct out of doors, without requesting permission?

The class was discussing the predominant themes in *Romeo and Juliet*, prior to reading the text.

Shakespeare, as you should know, is not on the syllabus for 4X. Shakespeare is reserved for academic pupils. Experimenting with the curriculum is not encouraged. Especially, I might add – Kilgore lowered his voice at this point – with students of this calibre.

He turned to his followers who had been listening to the exchange with eager curiosity. They were dressed in outfits appropriate for a prize-giving or graduation ceremony: the men wore light-weight suits; the women, linen dresses and jackets. Were they school inspectors, the board of governors, some kind of steering committee? Whoever they were, Kilgore was pulling out all the stops.

This is an unfortunate breach of regulations, he told them, which will not be repeated. Miss Price is a probationer who has not yet acclimatised herself to the ways of the department. She is a native of the Central Belt where, as we know, they do things differently. The visitors nodded knowingly and murmured amongst themselves. Right 4X, on your feet and back to your classroom, pronto! For the remainder of the afternoon you will draft letters of application for employment. These will be collected in by Miss Price and brought to me for inspection. And please, try to be realistic in your aspirations. I do not wish to read any letters applying for work as astrophysicists or brain surgeons.

The visitors tittered. 4X formed an almost orderly line and shambled back to Hut B.

Miss Price, see me at the end of the day.

Kilgore spun round on his polished brogues and flapped off towards the main building, his entourage trotting after him.

4X threw themselves into their seats.

Aw, Miss! Jockie gied ye a right dressin doon.

No way tae speak tae a teacher in front ae a class.

Specially this class!

Will ye get in trouble, Miss? Will they sack ye?

No. They won't sack me.

We could say we *made* ye tak us oot.

I doubt that would cut any ice with Mr Kilgore. I'm supposed to be in charge. We'd better make a start on those business letters. I'll put a template on the board. Just fill in the blanks.

Aw, Miss. Can we no read *Romeo and Juliet*?

4x's loyalty might have strengthened Gala's wavering commitment to the profession of teaching but Kilgore had persuaded her otherwise. At the end of the day, along with a crumpled stack of business letters, she was going to hand in her notice.

Clay

BY THE TIME he had taken up pottery and chucked in amateur dramatics and pipe smoking, Gala's father had built a studio onto the side of the house, hefted in a potter's wheel and a small kiln. A real studio at last, with a separate entrance, lock and key, and skylight window – privacy! Unless burglars were to climb on the roof and shimmy through the skylight, he was unassailable and out of sight.

The studio had a concrete floor and bare plaster walls. A thick film of clay dust soon covered everything: floors, work surfaces, his clothes, shoes, the record player, ashtray, the Dimple bottle. The imprint of his fingers marked coffee mugs, whisky glasses, records, especially Marlene's records, though now and again he did dust down her sleeve with a rag.

He grew a beard, rolled up his sleeves. He'd worked with clay before, when he was modelling heads, busts and figurines but now he was buying the stuff by the hundredweight, lugging damp slabs from the car boot, transporting it down the driveway by wheelbarrow to the garage which now functioned as his stockroom. His talk was of the advantages of terracotta over stoneware and vice versa, of slip and biscuit, of glazes, glazes and glazes, and problems with the kiln.

Though he knew a bit about clay, Miles had no previous experience of throwing pots, of glazing or firing them but decided to teach himself. He soon became aware that preparation for the interesting parts of pottery, the throwing, the glazing, the firing, were time-consuming and tedious. Impatient to see results, he offered Gala extra pocket money to clean up, stir the slip and, after detailed instructions, to mix some of the glazes. It was better than weeding. Jas complained bitterly. He'd have much preferred getting stuck in to the messy stuff with his father to inching around the herbaceous border, on the lookout for dandelions, but was, yet again, too young to be trusted to follow Miles's instructions to the letter.

Gala enjoyed watching his early and often disastrous attempts to throw pots. It was a tricky business. To make the wheel turn, which made the throwing plate turn, the foot bar had to be depressed repeatedly at a steady rhythm and a steady speed. When speed and rhythm were established and the plate was spinning like a long-playing record on the turntable, a lump of clay had to be thrown bang on the middle of the plate. Then and only then, the clay centred and firmly stuck, he cupped the lump with slip-lubricated hands, cupped it gently, let it spin inside his palms until it became a smooth, symmetrical mound. Then and only then, gently but firmly, he pushed his thumbs into the spinning mass of clay, pressed down, down until he had a smooth symmetrical hollow. Then, with fingers and thumbs, he squeezed outside and inside – gently, gently! – and gradually eased the spinning, hollow mound upwards and outwards.

If it went to plan, he got a pot. If it didn't, he got a disaster. The process was all concentration and control, all feeling his way into the clay, easing it, little by little. No sudden movements other than the initial slam against the plate. No distractions allowed. No taking his eye off the spinning ball of clay.

From the moment his foot hit the kick-bar until the wheel slowed down and clanked to a standstill, Gala was not permitted to speak or move. Marlene spun and crackled grittily during a throwing, at unusually low volume. The clay shimmered and quivered and rose up like some simple, throbbing life form, like a creature from the swamp.

When it worked, and a pot appeared – smooth, full-bellied,

symmetrical – her father's eyes flashed and glittered. When the tower of clay sagged and crumpled, had to be scraped off the plate and tossed in the bucketful of rejects for reconstitution, he cursed, paced and sucked furiously on one cigarette after another. If he had a run of disasters, he'd thump the work surface and tell her to go away and amuse herself elsewhere; to leave him be. Even still, she continued to hope that if she were patient and served her time fetching rags and tubs of glaze, stirring slip and listening to his far from expert words of advice and his curses when things didn't go to plan, one day he'd let her have a shot on the wheel.

A summer evening. Jas had been a pain, shaking the earth which clung to dandelion roots in her face when he was supposed to be doing his bit of the border. He just wanted to play; he always wanted to play and Gala wouldn't have minded but the weeding was never done. It was supposed to be fun having a garden but before you got to playing you had to pull up dandelions. And there were always more dandelions. Just when you thought you'd got the last one you'd see the tell-tale, toothed leaf of another, and another. Even if Gala could ignore the baby-toothed leaves pushing their way up through the earth, could kid herself that they might turn out to be some pretty flowers nobody had ever seen before, her mother would spot them, identify them for what they were. So she told Jas to grow up or get lost. After all, there was pocket money at stake.

When her share of the weeding was done, she dumped her stack of limp greenery on the compost heap and made her way to the studio. Her knees were pocked with dried mud, grass and crushed insects; she had stones in her sandals. But her father had promised. Over her shorts and Aertex shirt, she tied the strings of a clay-spattered apron which reached the floor. Cigarette smoke twirled upwards towards the skylight where an oblong of blue was steadily deepening. House martins looped. Later, imperceptibly, bats would take over the show.

The steps of an almost-learned tarantella tormented her toes. She had a dance show coming up. Her father turned

Marlene over, splashed some whisky in a dusty, clay-thumbed glass, knocked back a slug, cleared a space on the work counter and passed her a lump of clay. It was heavy, cool, smooth.

Put all your weight behind it. Press down – harder! Squeeze out all the air. Every last molecule. A single bubble and it won't work. A single bubble and it will blow up in the kiln –

I know that, Dad. I know about air bubbles. My head –

Let's not talk about your head.

She could feel a guilty smirk coming on and kept her eyes fixed on the lump of clay, the possible pot. The hated head, her head, which had been handed over to Chitti, back when she was little and still lived in the city, had never got as far as the furnace. It had exploded in Chitti's kiln, the pigtails and the sulk blown to smithereens. One wish had come true, and a bad wish at that.

You have to press harder. Let me show you how it's done.

I can do it. I can do it!

Let me show you how it's done.

He moved in and finished off kneading and squeezing and bashing until he was convinced there wasn't a drop of air inside the lump of clay.

Watch me. Look and learn.

But I've watched loads of times.

Watch again. I'm not doing this for my own entertainment.

He started up the wheel, demonstrating the kicking motion again:

Slow and steady. Put your full weight behind it, not just your leg.

Dance classes had strengthened Gala's leg muscles. Operating the kick-wheel was nothing compared to some ballet exercises.

I can do it! Look! I can do it! It's easy.

Is it, now? We'll see about that.

I mean the kicking. I can do kicking. My dance teacher says I've got good technique.

This isn't ballet. Ballet's got nothing to do with it. And operating the wheel is the easy bit. Let's see how you get on with centring.

She kept the kick-wheel going and held the clay above the plate. If she didn't think about what her foot was doing, what the wheel was doing and what the plate was doing, she could keep a steady rhythm going. She had to try not to think about it. It was like rubbing your belly and patting your head at the same time, you had to become automatic like a machine, to do it without thinking then once you were in your stride you had to throw the clay at the centre of the spinning plate and keep your foot going steadily –

That's no use! It's not centred. Foot off the wheel. Off the wheel!

He took the wire cutter, sliced the clay off the plate, slapped it down on the workbench and wiped down the plate with a damp rag.

Try again. Aim. Throw.

Perhaps she didn't have the aim, the strength, the confidence. Time and again she flung and missed the middle but if he hadn't watched her every move, if he'd just stood back for a minute, and looked away, she was sure she'd have got the hang of it. It was always hard to concentrate when somebody was watching. When the ballet teacher was staring at somebody else's feet, she could dance beautifully but when she watched Gala's feet, even the simplest *pas de chat* could go all wrong.

Her father was never one for standing back, looking away, letting his daughter learn from her mistakes. Did he think she'd have an accident, fall against the spinning plate and slice her face open, garotte herself with the wire he used to slice a finished piece off the plate?

In the end he centred the clay, then stood over, around, above as she stuck in her thumbs and pressed down, watching the hole grow deeper and feeling the wet clay whorl beneath her fingers. Handling the cool, silky clay felt so good that she forgot about the pot she was supposed to be throwing. And when the clay began to wobble, she laughed.

Concentrate! You've got to concentrate! He scraped off the mess, wiped down the wheel.

After several attempts she managed to produce a small,

lopsided thing which just might, at a pinch, pass for a pot. She drew the wire across the base, lifted it carefully off the plate and laid her effort alongside her father's sturdy, full-bodied vessels.

Can I try again?

That's enough for today.

Just once more, please?

Another day, perhaps.

Have I got talent? Have I got promise?

Off you go now.

He wiped his hands on his apron – which was stiff with paint and glaze and dried clay – lit another cigarette and turned up the volume on Marlene.

Will you fire my pot?

We'll see.

About a House

GRANNY AND GRANDAD Price lived in an old house, in the leafy midriff of England, in a village called Toombe. The village sat in a green cauldron of a valley which drew in all the country smells and cooked them up. The house stood in a lush garden which swayed down to a brook – a brook, not a burn – and smelled of lavender and honeysuckle. Sticky summer heat clung to everything. The hedgerows seethed with birds and insects. A weeping willow trailed the tips of its branches in the dancing water. Creamy hollyhocks, red hot pokers and languid delphiniums nodded in the faint, scented breeze. Somewhere, a country dog barked incessantly.

Blast that dog, said Grandad Price, without energy or enthusiasm.

Don't waste your breath complaining, Teddy, said Granny Price. It's in a dog's nature to bark.

Granny Price, whose name was Maud, though only Grandad ever called her that, was small and busy; she bustled. Her steely bun was secured with tortoiseshell combs. She wore a crisp blouse and a grey, fitted skirt which almost reached her ankles and made her bottom look as big and round and solid-looking as the fruit bowls her father had begun to turn out. When she bent to pull up a dandelion, or pick up her spectacles, which had a habit of falling off her nose, Jas gawped and sniggered. Granny

Price bustled but even when she was smiling and laughing, the deep cleft between her steely eyebrows never lifted.

Grandad Price was tall, stooped, silent. His hair was flat as dead grass, his eyes pale and watery. There were reasons for his silence but Gala and Jas were not to ask. They were to be on their best behaviour: to speak when spoken to; not to interrupt or make a nuisance of themselves; not to show off or ask too many questions. Especially about the war. Not that the war was foremost in Gala's mind. Elephants and tigers were much more interesting, and faraway places with sweet, spicy names and terrific stamps. Teddy Price had been a tea planter. Out East. Before the war. He didn't actually walk across the sloping terraces in the hill country, sowing seeds. He didn't actually pick tea leaves off the bushes either. Smiling brown ladies in saris did all that. On tea packets, little oval pictures showed the smiling ladies in the fields with baskets strapped to their foreheads, plucking tea leaves from shiny bushes. There was no sign of anybody who looked like Grandad but even though she was sure she knew the answer, Gala asked the question again.

Of course he didn't plant the tea himself! her father scoffed. Don't be ridiculous. Your grandfather was a manager. A supervisor, an overseer. He made sure the company got its money's worth out of the labour force. As I did when I was out there, working to pay for my brother and sister's education. The men are lackadaisical by nature, the women forever having babies. Not that they make a fuss about it, mind you. Just lie down in a ditch and get on with it. A woman who's given birth in the morning can be back at work the same afternoon. Still, somebody had to crack the whip or nothing would ever get done. And making others buckle down to work is not an easy job, I can tell you.

Did Grandad Price say anything other than *Blast that dog*? Granny Price did a lot of talking, mainly to Vera, in a high, spry voice, and mostly about Uncle Kenneth, who had a glass eye. Her words fluttered across the garden to where Gala was sketching lupins and their umbrella leaves.

The pain was terrible, Vera. You've no idea. I wouldn't wish such agony on my worst enemy – not even the Nips, I swear, even after all they put Teddy and me through – let alone my dear boy.

Gala didn't hear her say anything about Miles being her dear boy. It was Kenneth this and Kenneth that and if only Kenneth would and Kenneth really should and once Kenneth finally... Granny Price would die happy. How could that be?

And that husband of yours, Vera, has he settled yet? Has he seen sense and abandoned his harebrained notions?

Gala didn't catch her mother's reply but saw her squirm in her chair, square her shoulders and stick her chin in the air. When the breeze shifted and she could overhear no more, Gala skipped down the grassy slope to the brook where Jas was poking around, in search of frogs.

Uncle Kenneth's got a glass eye, said Gala.

What d'you mean?

One of his eyes is fake. It's glass that's been made to look like an eyeball.

Why?

Why what?

Why does he have a glass eye?

'Cos he lost one of his real ones, stupid.

He lost his eye?

He didn't really lose it. He had an accident.

What kind of accident?

How do I know? Something complicated. In an aeroplane factory. His eye didn't just fall out of its socket and drop down a drain. That can't happen. Your eyes are attached to your head. Otherwise every time you bent over they'd fall out, wouldn't they?

Jas tested the theory by sticking his head between his knees.

They had to take his eye out. The doctors. It was agony. You've no idea. You wouldn't wish such agony on your worst enemy.

Can you see with a glass eye?

Don't be stupid.

What's it for then?

So he doesn't have to wear a patch and look like a pirate. So he looks like a normal person.

Gala had never seen Uncle Kenneth and had no idea what he looked like. What interested her more was how anybody could work out which eye was real and which was glass. Her mother was always telling her to look people in the eye, that only a person with something to hide, who was shifty by nature, didn't look people in the eye. But how would you know which eye to look at? If you chose the glass one by mistake, that would be rude, like staring at somebody's pegleg, or a stump where there should be a finger.

Miles wandered down the garden, leaving Grandad Price sitting on his own, tapping the grass with his walking stick and cocking his ear at the sound of the barking dog.

There you are! I hope you're staying out of trouble.

Are we going to meet Uncle Kenneth? Jas asked, anxious but excited by the prospect of an encounter with a glass-eyed man.

I wouldn't worry about that, said her father. Uncle Kenneth is not likely to show his face while I'm here. We no longer see eye to eye.

He laughed without mirth. Jas thought his father had made a great joke and laughed so much he began to hiccup. Gala slapped Jas on the back to stop the hiccups and got a clip round the ear from her father.

Tarnish

ON DAYS WHICH have not been shelved in the memory with a cross, a black mark or any other signifier, Grandad Price died, then Granny Price died. Gala did not attend either funeral. She is not sure whether or not her father made the journey to Toombe. What she does remember is that, when she was alive, Granny Price had a bad back. Which had something to do with the Japanese. She had been put in traction, which Gran explained was a kind of stretching, straightening procedure.

Sounds like torture!

Dinny joke about torture! Gran replied, in an uncharacteristically sharp tone, and continued scraping potatoes.

Because of her bad back, Granny Price had slept on a board. She carried one around with her, a portable, folding contraption with flaps and hinges. If she'd come to visit, Gala would have remembered the bed board. Did Granny and Grandad Price ever make the trip north to see Miles, their firstborn, in his own home with his own family?

At some point after Granny Price's death, a will was read, in a solicitor's office. And the will made Gala's father angry. Very angry. Hopping mad. For a long time. Possibly the rest of his life. He and Vera didn't get the house, not even a share of it, but neither did Uncle Kenneth who had gone through terrible pain and become an incomplete human being. Gala's parents were, however, sent some tea chests which contained, amongst other things, a dusty sari, a turban and a dozen silver teaspoons beaten into intricate leaf shapes, which lay in a box padded with Prussian blue velvet.

Too fancy for everyday use, said her mother, glancing at the teaspoons. And by the looks of them, not much good for stirring up anything but trouble. As for the finely wrought but damaged jewelry box, she said: I might have known there would be something wrong with it.

At the bottom of the chests, thrown in higgledy-piggledy, a jumble of tarnished metal plates and a circular table top, intended to rest on a low-legged wooden frame, rubbed up against each other like the sort of stuff going for a song at the Barras.

Would you credit the state of it all, Miles? said her mother. Does that sister of yours think we have skivvies to do our dirty work? She might have had the decency to clean the damn stuff, given all the time she has on her hands.

Ye never know, said Gran. A right bobby-dazzler might lie beneath aw yon tarnish.

If there was anything of value in there, her mother continued, believe you me, Angela wouldn't have parted with it.

Gran bent down and peered into the cupboard under the sink where all the cleaning fluids were kept.

Sometimes, Vera, ye're just too high and mighty for yir ain good.

Vera flounced off in a huff. Miles lit a cigarette and made for the studio. Strains of Marlene began to seep through the walls. Jas, who had no interest in old junk, left Gala and Gran in the kitchen with the open tea chests. Gran rolled up her sleeves, put on her pinny and set to tackling years of neglect, hoping to put a shine on what was now and ever more would be a tarnished memory.

Gala unravelled the sari and began to wind it around her waist. It was stiff and waxy, intricately patterned in burnt sienna and indigo on a background of ochre. It smelled of candles and cinnamon.

There's tons of this stuff.

Aye an if ye keep goin like yon, ye'll end up swaddled like a Mummy. Pit it away the now. Keep it clear o the muck that's comin oot these plates.

Reluctantly, Gala unwound the sari and folded it up.

Why did the Egyptians make Mummies?

Tae preserve their deid. The Egyptians were gey knowledgeable aboot embalming.

Why did they want to preserve dead bodies?

So they could look their best in the hereafter. Aw the right preparations had tae be made.

Do you believe in the hereafter?

I'm no sure I believe in this life, never mind anither yin! But look here, d'you see? Gran held up a filthy plate with equally filthy hands. An elephant! And a fella wi eight airms!

Up close, the sharp smell of Brasso prickled Gala's nostrils. On the surface of the blackened dish a silvery outline of an elephant was emerging from the tarnish which, now that it was loosening, was the deepest, darkest black imaginable, so dark it was bright, the way ice was so cold it could burn. On the other plate a creature, half human, half octopus, was twirling many arms and wiggling its hips: dancing. Gran held up another plate.

Whit d'ye think we'll find on this yin?

Patience, said Gran, applying more Brasso and elbow grease. Look again, ye o little faith.

The tarnish began to soak through the rag and there, beneath Gran's work-worn fingers, a skinny, long-legged bird picked its way through tall rushes.

Is it a flamingo?

Too big a beak. An ibis, mibbe. The ibis wis special for the Egyptians.

With each wipe of the rag, the bird became more distinct; every feather had been picked out in silver. Cleaning, at least that day, was a kind of magic.

Can I try?

Put on a pinny, then. Cleaning's dirty work. Look at me. I'm dirtier than Jock the coalman.

Gran was on friendly terms with all the tradespeople who

called by the house: the coalman, whose full name was Jeremiah Clough; the Onion Johnny, Monsieur Claude Simenon; Frank Featherstone, the Kleeneze man, who sold dusters and brushes, tins of polish and wax, salts and soaps, emollients and abrasives; Tommy Turner, the ragman who slung old clothes and torn curtains onto his cart; and Anastasia, the gypsy with the baby on her back, from whom Gran regularly bought crocheted tea cosies and antimacassars because the poor soul was trying her best.

Gala's mother only dealt with Mr Woolf, the piano tuner, and the fish man who was only ever called the fish man.

Try this yin, said Gran, handing over a small, blackened disc. Mibbe it'll mak a nice wee ashtray for yir faither. He can aye use anither ashtray.

It was thin as a tin lid but once the tarnish began to dissolve Gala could feel a raised texture through the soft cloth. The Brasso was a dirty yellow – something between Naples Yellow and grey – and the fumes made her light-headed. Slowly but surely a gleam of silver began to emerge from the filth.

It's got writing on it.

So it has.

It took a while until all the words were legible: *For Edward Price, in recognition of his part in the annual tug of war. Bandung, 1941.*

Dear, dear, said Gran. 1941. Bandung. To think Angela let that go. Let's hope yir faither will be pleased tae hae it. Mak it as bright as ye can. Keep on polishin till ye can see yir face in it.

By the time they were done they had used up a heap of rags and their arms were black to the elbows. The tarnish soaked deep into the skin, as if being lifted from the plates, it had to find somewhere else to make its mark. They scrubbed their arms until they were pink and stinging, dipped the metal plates in hot soapy water, rinsed them clean then set them on the sideboard –suns and moons which held on their shining disks an exotic array of flora and fauna.

Miles came into the kitchen, caked in clay dust, in search of a box of matches.

Look, Dad! Grandad was in a tug of war. In Bandung! Look!

He turned the shimmering thing round and round. Blades of light flashed around the kitchen.

Well, well, he said. Wondered where that went to.

He picked up a couple of other plates, turned them over, inspected the hallmarks.

Indian silver, he said. Won't be worth much.

The plates were hung on the sitting room wall above the circular coffee table which turned out to be copper, inlaid with silver hieroglyphs and figures from Egyptian mythology. The heirlooms were often remarked on by visitors and parents of Vera's piano pupils. The fine craftsmanship from faraway and long ago hinted at an elegant, sumptuous lifestyle. Vera dismissed the compliments with patently false modesty: *Just a trifle they picked up on their travels* – as if the Price family had been a band of intrepid explorers. Later, she would relate to Miles that some parent who was a doctor or lawyer had singled out this piece or that for praise. Miles ignored her.

The coffee table was particularly admired but never used. It had short legs and was intended to be surrounded by floor cushions. Gala and Jas were all for getting some cushions.

Nobody's going to be sitting around like Arabs in this house, said Miles, who barely looked at the stuff, though the tug of war ashtray found its way to the studio and was permanently littered with fag ends.

From the moment he found out that he had been stiffed by the will – cheated, he declared, of his rightful inheritance, he who'd given years of his life so his younger brother and sister could finish their education, he who'd not had an ounce of support when he struck out as an artist – dissatisfaction rumbled through the house like a gathering storm, never quite coming to a head, never quite passing over.

Splitting Hairs

FOR MOST OF the morning, Mrs Brockley had been marking the end of term test. She had given the class a book to read, a long, slow story which wasn't very exciting, even if it did have pirates and parrots and treasure. Mrs Brockley was as old and tough as a turnip left out for the sheep but she rarely missed a trick. She would appear to be deep in marking, some gullible pupil would take the opportunity of whispering to a neighbour and before the culprit could govern his or her tongue, Mrs Brockley's chalky hand slammed down on her desk.

Does nobody in this class comprehend what silence means?

By the end of the morning she had given out a string of black marks and the boy sitting next to Gala was going to get the belt if she caught him out again. She ordered the class to sit still and silent while she went through the test papers, red pencil swooping on one script after another, ticking and crossing, sighing and tutting, shaking her boxy head and scratching her lilac nose. The air crackled with suspense. When the lunch bell rang the class filed out, sidling close to the teacher's desk, hoping for a squint at the mark sheet but Mrs Brockley's arm strategically covered all intelligence. When she left the classroom, however, she was empty-handed.

In the dinner hall the talk was of nothing but the test. Brockley had tormented them all, marking papers in front of their very eyes and everybody wanted to know their score that very minute. When the sponge pudding and custard were done, Gala left the dinner hall, slipped up the wide wooden stairs, along the deserted corridor and into the unlocked classroom where the test papers lay on the teacher's desk like temptation itself. Had somebody dared her, had she dared herself, or simply become impatient with the endless speculation? She can't remember. Heart thumping, ears primed for the sound of approaching footsteps, she scanned the mark sheet, memorised what she could of names and numbers and left.

Back in the playground, without a moment's hesitation, she related her findings. The mark sheet was incomplete so she couldn't satisfy everybody and, to avoid being the bringer of bad news, withheld the very lowest marks. When it was time to line up and troop back to the classroom, the entire class was fizzing like lightbulbs ready to pop. Mrs Brockley waited until everyone had settled down before going in for the kill.

During the lunch hour, she said, lingering over every word as if the class were supposed to memorise it, somebody came into *my* classroom – which, as you all know is against the rules – and *tampered* with the *test papers*.

A strangled gasp went around the room. Gala's blood ran hot, cold, hot. She shrank back into her seat. How did Brockley know? Nobody had seen her go in. She had checked that the coast was clear, been extra careful, that had been part of the challenge, slipping in and out undetected, like a good spy.

I expect somebody in this room is wondering how I know, said Mrs Brockley, as if all Gala's thoughts were written on the blackboard in capital letters. Well, I'll tell you. I set a little trap. Across the papers, I laid a couple of hairs. Which are no longer there. So unless a mouse scampered over my desk and dislodged them, *somebody* has *tampered* with the *test papers*!

A trap! And Gala had walked right into it.

This is a very serious matter. As some papers were not yet marked, whoever tampered with them could quite easily have *cheated*. We shall sit here until somebody owns up. If nobody owns up, the whole class will be *punished*.

The silence in the room was thick and heavy. Gala was scared, very scared. Nobody was glancing anywhere near her which was somehow worse than if they'd all pointed the finger. It had never occurred to her to cheat. Why did the old bag have to make things worse? After a brief, tense pause, Gala declared in a faint, wobbling voice that she was the one, that she'd only looked. The fact remained, Mrs Brockley insisted, that she *could have changed an answer,* she *might have thought about cheating.*

After an eternity of quaking outside the headmaster's door, palms running rivers of sweat, heart throwing itself against her ribs like a trapped rabbit, the green *Enter* sign flashed. From the far side of his broad mahogany desk, the headmaster, a large, looming man in a black gown, delivered a stern lecture, a lengthy punishment exercise and worse, much worse, a letter home.

Of course she confessed straight away, sobbing and gulping into Gran's pinny, and Gran believed that she hadn't meant to cheat, she was clever enough to get good marks without cheating, wasn't she, she was a clever girl and most of the time a good girl and one telling off in a day was enough to be going on with and in the midst of all her weeping and wailing Gala wondered how bad something she'd done would have to be before Gran turned against her. But the letter home wasn't addressed to Gran.

Mrs Brockley says Gala might have cheated, her mother announced the moment her father came in the door, before he'd even had a chance to pour himself a whisky, light a cigarette, or complain about his working day, about his efforts to instil discipline into lazy incompetent pupils, before he'd even had time to put down the briefcase, in which he carried his strap.

Gala had already explained repeatedly to her mother that she hadn't cheated so why did she have to bring it up straight away? She went through it all over again, as if she were being cross-examined for a murder: she'd only looked, hadn't changed a thing, hadn't even thought about cheating. And she'd owned up. She'd been brave and honest and saved the whole class from a punishment exercise. But with Gala's parents there was no escape from the rules of school, from their unwavering belief that Teacher Knows Best, and in the lessons that should be learned from punishment.

This hurts me more than you, her father said, raising the strap. Hold out your hands.

Her mother stood by, made no attempt to intervene. Were her arms folded? Was the look on her face one of resignation or grim approval? It certainly wasn't one of sympathy. When Gala held out her trembling hands and waited for pain, she believed, fervently, and still does, that what her father said in justification of his action, was a lie. And it was not so much the pain – though for hours her hands felt as if she'd stuck them in the fire – but the injustice which burned and went on burning.

Surf & Turf

BEGUN ON THE back of a postcard which features a still from the 1974 film of *The Great Gatsby*, starring Mia Farrow and Robert Redford, both looking bleached and angelic, and continued on airmail notepaper:

Dear Mum and Dad,
Sorry it's taken a while for me to get around to
writing but the days have just raced by. New York is
crazy. The streets are like long deep canyons and the sky
is very far away. Everything moves so fast it's like being
on the big dipper. The taxis and police cars screech by
and there are hundreds of people everywhere you look,
at all times of day and night, all trying to get on, to get
ahead of the next guy, all talking nineteen to the dozen,
yelling above the traffic noise. If you get in somebody's
way, if you're not walking fast enough, they can be
pretty rude. I only stayed three nights and I hardly slept
at all it was so noisy. I booked a cheap hotel at the
airport which was very central, just off Times Square.
On my last day in the Big Apple, I went to Coney
Island which is like an old fairground by the sea, with
hot dog stalls and sideshows and rollercoasters. The
beach was chock-a-block with people. Even in the

water it was standing room only. It was so weird. Folk were just standing there, up to the waist in water, eating monster ice creams and submarine sandwiches, which are a foot long, I'm not kidding, and completely stuffed with filling. There's one sandwich you can buy which has about half a pound of rare roast beef in it. It's called a Wounded Elephant – can you imagine ordering a Wounded Elephant? With mustard? I did some drawing at Coney Island. Lots to look at!

I'm in N – now, and glad to be somewhere quieter. I'm staying with Cath Crombie. She's the older sister of a friend from home, a good bit older, married – well, separated – with twin teenage daughters, Patty and Franny, who are really hard to tell apart. Cath has made me very welcome and introduced me to tons of people. It's good to stay with somebody. It saves money but it's also a better way to see how people live here, from the inside.

The town is on the coast and by American standards historical. A few buildings date back to the 17th century, wooden houses with porches and verandas, painted in pastel colours, sort of toytown but pretty. And out on The Drive are all kinds of fancy mansions. People with money to burn have built their own dream homes so there's a neo-gothic monstrosity next to a rococo confection next to a modernist glass and steel polyhedron. You can go on a guided tour of and get the lowdown on all the famous people who've lived there but Cath has let me in on the gossip about most of them already so no need for a tour!

Quite a few of the mansions have been used as locations for movies. Cath's kids were extras in The Great Gatsby. *The straw hats they wore on set are now on Cath's mantelpiece, as well as signed photos of the stars. Cath knows everybody and there's always a party on the go. It's a wonder anybody ever gets any work done. Most people I've met through her are in business*

*of some kind, working for themselves. Cath herself is
very popular and stylish and looks really young for her
age. She has a lovely apartment (flat), and a collection
of art deco glass which she dusts every day. She used
to have a job with a party planning company but
quit after a disagreement with her boss. She's looking
around for other work but for the moment she has
plenty time to show me around. We're often invited out
for dinner. You should see the meals people cook here
– steak, jumbo shrimp, lobster with all kinds of fancy
sauces. Cath's friends like to splash out but I'm not
complaining!*

*The town is a big sailing place. Some yachts moored
in the marina cost more than houses. The weather has
been good and I've got a bit of a tan but nothing like the
locals, who take their sunbathing very seriously. The sea
is warmer than at home – quite a lot warmer! – and there
are some nice beaches but a lot of them are private so
you can't just go for a walk along the coast. I don't think
people should be able to buy up bits of coastline but here
you can buy anything you want, if you have the money.*

*Hope things are okay with everybody. I wasn't
planning to stay here more than a couple of weeks but
Cath keeps finding more for us to do and more people
to meet!*

Love from Gala, xx

What didn't go in the letter was that, as well as being
unemployed, Cath Crombie was recently divorced from a hard
drinking, bent out of shape, old school redneck who showed
up every so often and threatened boots upside the head for
whoever happened to cross his skewed line of vision. More
mouth than muscle, if Cath's testimony was reliable, but even
so, his last visit had upset the twins. The custody arrangement
allowed their father access every other weekend but he wanted
to see them as and when the mood took him. And it tended to
take him after he'd had a skinful.

Cath had pasted a photo of her ex-husband to the fridge door and given Gala instructions that under no circumstances was he to be allowed into the apartment. Unless he'd joined AA or was delivering an alimony cheque. He'd been behind with payments for months. Lack of alimony and Cath's misunderstanding with her boss meant that she was in serious rent arrears. Her lovely apartment was about to be repossessed unless somebody bailed her out very soon.

Welfare cheques and food stamps helped keep the wolf from Cath's door, as did a couple of nights a week moonlighting in a gay bar. Cath found it hard to accept her reduced circumstances and identify with the poor and needy, preferring to spend her food stamps on jumbo shrimp and filet mignon on offer than find a hundred and one ways to cook hamburger. To help out, the twins worked a few shifts in a waterfront restaurant. Gala chipped in at the supermarket checkout and wondered, given Cath's extravagant tastes, how far her limited budget was likely to stretch.

Dinner invitations also helped out and in Cath's strategy for survival, Gala acted as a chaperone of sorts. Cath knew a number of older men; widowers, divorcees, even a couple of married men whose wives took long vacations in the Virgin Islands and other Caribbean hotspots. These men liked to show off their culinary expertise, prided themselves on sourcing the finest ingredients and keeping the booze flowing; cocktails, fine wines, after dinner drinks followed on occasion by a little pot, a line or two, hilarity and sexual innuendo. Cath lived on her wit and her wits, and never forgot to pre-book a taxi home.

Swipe!

AS THE OLD money didn't materialise, Gala's father began to dream up ways to bring in the new. One Saturday morning he went off to pay a man a visit and came home with a light in his eye and a bootload of cardboard boxes.

This, he said, if I play my cards right, could make me a packet! Go and fetch your mother.

Her mother was at the bottom of the garden, yanking weeds out of the rose bed and tossing them onto a limp heap.

What is it this time?

I don't know. But there's lots of boxes.

She dropped her trowel and sighed.

Right, said Miles, loud and clear and wound up. Gather round.

He opened two boxes. One held a score of plastic bottles filled with a turquoise liquid, the other a similar number of spray guns. With a flourish, he held up a bottle of liquid and a spray gun.

What we have here is *Swipe!* A brand new miracle cleaner. It's been doing very well over in America but isn't widely available here. Yet. But when it is, you can bet your bottom dollar, people will be climbing over each other to get their hands on it. Very easy to use. Cleans just about anything. Put some concentrate in the spray gun, add water, give it a good shake and you're in business. Now take a look at it in action.

He poured some concentrate into a spray gun, filled it up with water and gave it a shake. He held up a tray covered with blobs of hardened paint and clay, scooshed on some *Swipe!* and began to wipe it off. The clay dissolved quickly. The paint took a bit longer.

There! What do you think of that? Safe for kitchen and bathroom, for woodwork, paint and plastic. One product does all. That's the beauty of it. No point in having a cupboard full of different cleaners. All you need is *Swipe!* Wipe on *Swipe! Swipe!* off grime!

Wipe on *Swipe! Swipe!* off grime! Jas chanted.

This is what people want. Something quick and easy and economical. No waste. What do you think, Vera? After seeing my demonstration, you'll use it, won't you?

I might.

And you, Gran?

I'll certainly gie it a try, Miles.

That's the spirit!

But what are we going to do with so much of it? Vera asked.

Sell it! I, or rather, *we* will act as selling agents. And if I play my cards right, we could do rather nicely out of it.

You're surely not intending to go door to door?

What do you take me for, some kind of Kleeneze man? I'm talking about pyramid selling. Pyramid selling! Do you know what that is?

Sounds like a racket to me, said Vera. And racketeers always come a cropper.

Well that shows how much you know. Pyramid selling is going to be the next big thing. The next big thing! What I have to do is identify a number of suitable clients, people with the right connections who are interested in buying into the scheme. I purchase so many boxes at such and such a rate and flog them at a higher rate and then –

You've already bought them.

You're stating the obvious, Vera. I had to act quickly. The offer was only available for a limited time. To a limited number of people. The company doesn't sell to just anybody, you know. It's discriminating. It is only interested in representatives of a certain calibre. What we need to do now is approach our contacts – friends, acquaintances, your pupils' parents, and so on. Test the water.

You want to me to sell a cleaning product to the parents of my piano pupils?

It's a quality product. For quality people. And you, Gran, tell your lady friends about it. We need to persuade as many contacts as we can to buy, from me, at a small discount, of course, then they can sell on to their own contacts and so on down the line. It's really very straightforward. We could make a killing if we can shift the stuff in bulk. I'm counting on all of you to talk it up to your friends. The versatility of the product, how economical it is, how much of a bargain it is, if they buy in bulk, and who to get it from. So keep the name in mind – *Swipe!*

I'd like to know, said Vera, who talked you into this.

Chap I met at the Gryffon. Stood me a couple of drinks and gave me the lowdown. Claims he's already made a mint himself. Been all over the country, identifying suitable representatives. Not just anybody can do this kind of thing successfully, you know. He's had years of experience in the business. Can tell a good agent when he sees one.

I might have known drink was involved.

In business, Vera, it's the way deals are done. You really don't have a clue about how the business fraternity operates.

If it involves giving credence to the spiel of half-cut wideboys, I've no wish to find out.

Vera was teetotal and had no time for alcohol-induced jollity, let alone alcohol-induced financial decisions. She did try to interest a few friends and some parents of her piano pupils in the product, though not the doctor, or the solicitor. Gran's few surviving friends lived frugally and had managed with their old faithful cleaning methods for more than half a century. And didn't fancy the sound of a spray gun. Occasionally, visiting a friend's house, Gala dutifully mentioned *Swipe!* but avoided embarking on the ins and outs of pyramid selling.

As for her father, he was never so outgoing, amenable or sociable as when he had a spray gun of *Swipe!* in his hands and a sales pitch running. Neighbours to whom, under other circumstances, he would usually offer the most curt and dismissive of nods, he'd buttonhole on the street, inquire after their spouses, kids, dogs, cars, gardens, hedges, fences, keeping the chit-chat going until he could introduce his topic of the moment – *Swipe!*

His eyes were bright, too bright, his dentured grin too wide. He took on the role of salesman as easily as that of a stage villain. Convinced that he had the gift of the gab and could charm complete strangers into shelling out for the product, he might even have gone door to door had Vera not put her foot down about him lowering the tone of the family. He did sell some of the stuff. One or two, or three or four people bought small quantities of the cleaner, more out of kindness or embarrassment than because they were overcome by the seductive power of pyramid selling.

When it became apparent that friends, colleagues and acquaintances didn't jump at the chance to buy into a block of Miles Price's pyramid, he took their refusal to invest as a personal rejection. As if he'd counted on them all along. As if they'd promised some kind of commitment and then reneged on their promise. The unsold boxes of concentrate were moved from the kitchen cupboards to the back of the garage. For years Gran used it up as best she could. *Swipe!* cleaned things well enough.

Diversion

Exaggerate
Embarrass
Necessitate
Excessive
Possessive
Aggressive

SO, SAID HER father, you fancy yourself as an artist, do you?

The spelling was difficult, Gala had a test the following day and her new teacher, Miss Crake, considered accuracy in spelling to be one of the higher virtues.

Take a look at this. See what you can do with it. Keep away from the main part of the board. And the boxes where the mystery *Accident* cards will go. Leave them for now. Only use the empty space, is that clear? It's just a mock-up so you can please yourself how you fill it.

What do you want me to draw?

Something appropriate to a board game about motoring. It's going to be called Diversion. Good name, don't you think?

It's, yes, it's –

It's an excellent name. But you're probably not observant enough to appreciate the fact. Everybody who has to drive on the roads knows what a diversion is. They see the signs. So in effect I'll reap the benefit of free advertising all over the place.

Imagine. All that free advertising! I've really hit on something! Diversion could really catch on!

He was in his glitter-eyed, excitable state. The cigarette was sucked down, the floor pacing was accelerated. The whisky was a perpetual golden swirl in a perpetually adjacent tumbler. It was best to go along with what he wanted.

Oh, and remember to put the name of the game on the board. In big clear letters. Has to be easy to read. Nothing too fancy.

Exaggerate: Two Gs One R. Why? Embarrass. Two Rs Two Ss. No sense to it.

I'll leave it with you. See you what you can come up with. Nice bold motifs. Emblematic.

What does emblematic mean?

Never mind. Just keep it simple. I've done all the essential stuff. All I'm asking you to do is brighten up some empty space. You can manage that, can't you?

So far the board was just a big sheet of jotter blue sugar paper on which her father had drawn a main road and several side roads. Some of the side roads wound around for a while then rejoined the main road. Others were cul-de-sacs. There were traffic lights, T-junctions, crossroads and a roundabout. The board was divided into boxes like Monopoly. Just before every fork or junction or crossroad was a box marked D.

Is D for Diversion?

Of course it is. What else would it be for?

Ditch? Drop? Danger?

Don't try to be smart. While you're working on the background, think of some interesting diversions. I'll be needing a whole set of them. When you land on D, you'll turn up a card and find out why you have been diverted.

A runaway horse from a milk lorry? An overturned fruit barrow? An escaped tiger from the zoo?

That sort of thing, yes. But nothing too fanciful. More likely a flood, an accident, a tram derailment. We need *credible* diversions. Otherwise people won't take the game seriously.

Striking shipyard workers blocking the road?

No, no. We'll not be having any of that. Nobody wants that.

Gran says the workers are right to strike.

Not in my game they aren't.

What about a Ban the Bomb march? A peace protest?

Not on your nelly. Bunch of namby-pamby pacifists who don't know what it is to defend their country. This is a game. It's an *entertainment*. About driving. Is that clear? It's not going to be some kind of political soapbox.

He stubbed out his cigarette, lit another and paced.

Where are the roads meant to be?

It doesn't matter. It's a game. The aim of the game is to get to the end of the road.

But I can't think of what to draw unless I know where the roads are. Is it a city?

Of course it's a city. You don't have traffic lights in the country. Or roundabouts. Or cul-de-sacs, for that matter.

What city is it?

I've already said it doesn't matter. Any city. Just put in some houses, churches, police stations, courthouses, that kind of thing.

Could it be Paris? I could draw the Eiffel Tower, Notre Dame Cathedral, the Arc de Triomphe, the Moulin Rouge.

Gala had been doing a school project on Paris and the teacher had brought in pictures of all the famous landmarks. In all the photos there was a warm, golden quality to the light that she'd never seen in Glasgow, or anywhere else in Scotland.

You certainly won't be putting the Moulin Rouge on any board of mine. This is a game for all the family.

Miss Crake said Moulin Rouge meant Red Windmill.

Miss Crake has no right mentioning the Moulin Rouge at all. Take my word for it, it's not the sort of thing I want on my board. I doubt you have the technical expertise, the draughtsmanship to replicate a windmill. Besides, in France they drive on the wrong side of the road.

Didn't you and Mum go to Paris on your honeymoon?

We did. Your mother was more interested in inspecting lavatories than seeing the sights.

Maybe I'll just make up a city, said Gala.

You do that. And don't take too long over it. I want to conduct a trial run tonight, with the family, when your mother's pupils have eventually all gone home.

The bell rang. The front door opened. A flurry of *hellos* and *goodbyes*. The door shut.

That should be the last one going in now, so see what you can achieve in the next half hour. Remember it's just a mock-up.

Even though her father had been against a Parisian setting, Gala decided to use what little she knew of it as a basis: tree-lined avenues, elegant parks, fountains, statues. So as not to interfere with the road system in any way, she put bridges over rivers and arches over the entranceways to parks. She was still thinking about what kind of buildings to include when the last piano pupil left, the front door was shut firmly and her father came striding into the living room.

Right, let's get everything set up.

I'm not quite finished, said Gala.

He glanced at her efforts.

It's meant to be Paris, she said. Without the Moulin Rouge.

Looks more like airy-fairyland to me. But it'll have to do for now.

He coralled everyone in the dinette and spread the 'board' on the table.

Lovely trees, said Gran.

Gala did them, said Jas. I can't do trees yet.

I thought so. Yir sister's very clever wi a pencil.

Did you do your spelling? Her mother asked.

Yes but it was really hard.

You should have spent more time on it, then. If a thing's worth doing, it's worth doing well. Don't you have a test tomorrow?

Yes but Dad wanted me to –

Can we get on? said Miles.

He explained the basic idea of the game. Everybody was given a counter. In the finished version these would be miniature cars but for the moment they'd have to make do with Jas's collection of plastic models which came free in Cornflakes packets: a car, a rocket, a green spaceman, a blue spaceman and Bugs Bunny.

I want the car, said Jas.

I want doesn't get, said Vera.

Give him the bloody car, said Miles.

Language, said Vera.

We could use tiddlywinks instead, said Gran. They'd fit on the squares better.

How can a tiddlywink be a car? said Jas. That's stupid.

Don't call your gran stupid, said Vera.

A tiddlywink is round. Cars aren't round, said Jas.

Are we going to play this damn game or not? said Miles.

No need to get shirty, said Vera. By the way, it'll soon be the children's bedtime.

If it weren't for your piano pupils taking up most of the evening, we could have got started a whole lot earlier.

If it weren't for my piano pupils, we'd be a whole lot worse off.

Your piano pupils bring in pin money, Vera. I'm the one who brings home the bacon. I'm the one who has to teach, day in day out, and squeeze my artistic ambitions into spare moments.

Gran sat patiently, waiting for the bickering to be over, to get started, to get on, for the game to be over and done with so she could get back to doing something useful.

Diversion was slow to play. It had too many obstacles, too many stops and starts, too many diversions. Jas got restless and began fiddling with the counters, pushing them off their squares. Gala began adding statues to the parks.

Concentrate, the pair of you. Inventing a board game is a serious business.

I don't like serious business games, said Jas. I like good fun games.

You'll like what you get, said Miles.

Any more cheek and you'll be sent to bed without any cocoa, said Vera.

Look! said Gran, Silly me. I've landed on a D. Now, whit's

my penalty? Could ye read it for me, Jas, there's a good boy. My old eyes are no as good as your nice bright young ones.

Hit. By. A. Fallen. Tree. Miss. A. Turn.

Dearie me, just my luck. So who's in the lead now? The car. Who has the car?

Me, said Jas. I'm in the lead!

Can nobody in this house just play a simple game without all this shilly-shallying? I'm not doing this for my own entertainment. I'm planning to patent the thing. It could make a bomb. In a year's time it could be what everybody wants for Christmas but my own blasted family can't even help me to test drive it without causing an obstruction at every step of the way!

While he continued his harangue, Gala began to add a few extra blossom trees to the main boulevard. Her father snatched the cerise pencil from her hand and snapped it in two.

That's my favourite colour!

Make you think twice about not paying attention when I'm talking, then.

She stared so hard at the blue paper that the pink cherry trees began to sway.

Game over. You can go back to whatever you were doing, he said. If I can't rely on my own family for assistance, I'll work the thing out by myself. When this is in the shops and all your friends are meeting up for a game of Diversion, just remember, not one of you did a thing to help.

He swept up the cards and counters, rolled up the blue sugar paper.

I did the background, said Gala, the words scraping over the rocks in her throat. I helped.

That's as may be. But it's not what I asked for. I wanted a proper cityscape. No point in helping if you can't do what you're asked.

Fairways, Roughs and Bunkers

AND THEN THERE was golf. From spring to autumn, in anything but the worst weather, Gala's father was off to the golf course two or three evenings a week, eager to be out of the house and away from plodding piano scales, to focus on his swing, his driving, chipping and putting, and find ways to lower his handicap. Of course it wasn't all fresh air and exercise. After the round of golf came the round or three of drinks in the nineteenth hole, accompanied by cigarettes and an in-depth post-mortem on the game. And bragging, bluster, banter and oneupmanship. And conviviality. And bonhomie. A door had opened. He was meeting the right people now. Making connections. Only a matter of time before it would pay off.

When, after much wear and tear on her own and everybody else's nervous system, Gala's mother finally succeeded in passing her driving test, she began to drive Miles to the club on evenings when she had no piano pupils. Not that she enjoyed sitting around waiting in the car, wondering if a distant speck on the fairway was her husband or some other man still with several holes to play.

Vera suspected that on some occasions he told her he was held up on the course when he was already ensconced in the clubhouse, knocking back one more for the road and turning a blind eye to the wall clock. Resenting the time and the money he spent in the clubhouse, and the time she spent waiting for him to finally emerge, she came up with a plan. She bought her husband three tangerine golf jerseys. They were brighter than the flags which marked the holes.

I believe the colour is very much in vogue, Miles. And, as an artist, won't people expect you to keep up with colour trends?

True enough, he said. A conversation piece. Something to get them talking in the clubhouse.

When Miles eventually got wise to his wife's ruse, he opted for less conspicuous colours and Vera was once again reduced to waiting in irritable ignorance.

But why all the subterfuge? Why didn't Vera just let him drive himself to the clubhouse and come home when he was ready? Or poke her head into the bar, see whether he was there and haul him out? No, Vera wouldn't lower herself to such unseemly behaviour as dragging her husband out of a bar.

Around the same time as her father took up golf, Gala began piano lessons with Mrs Hammond, a brisk woman with a Brillo Pad of curls, bottle glasses and short plump fingers which appeared to double in length when she played octave chords. Mrs Hammond lived at the other end of the town, near the mental hospital, which had high walls and locked gates.

The hospital grounds ran alongside the roundabout which taxed Vera's road sense every time she encountered it. More often than not, she would drive twice round the roundabout before selecting the correct exit. The mental hospital was a talking point. Rumours went around about strange goings-on behind the walls, new-fangled practices and maverick shrinks, about rumpus rooms and loonies embracing their madness, about the distinction between doctors and patients being blurred.

Nobody asked Gala if she wanted to take up the piano. It was a chore having to do the practice but at least her mother wasn't her teacher. As it was, more than enough teaching went on around the Price house. When the L-plates first went on the Hillman Minx, Miles had insisted on taking Vera out for driving lessons. It would save money, he'd said, and besides, he knew all anybody needed to know about driving. But even before they'd left the driveway, the pair of them were sniping away at each other: *You should have/You shouldn't have/If you'd only told me/I did what you asked/How was I supposed to know?/It's only common sense/Easy for you to say.*

Dearie me, Gran would say, drying the dishes and watching from the kitchen window as the car hiccupped up the driveway. Trials and tribulations.

When Miles and Vera had returned from a lesson, the black Hillman Minx with silver trim grumbled into the drive. Car doors opened. Car doors slammed shut. Lips pursed. Brows furrowed. Scowls set like cement. It was only when Miles agreed, for the sake of everyone's nerves, especially his own, to shell out on a driving instructor – a patient, pessimistic man who spoke no more than absolutely necessary – that Vera began to get the hang of coordinating ignition, choke, clutch, accelerator and brake, and had the glimmer of a chance of passing her driving test.

When Miles took up golf he bought Jas some miniature clubs and tried to teach his son what little he knew about upswing and downswing, about keeping your eye on the ball and following through. Jas obligingly hacked divots from the lawn, pitched balls into the next door neighbours' garden. He didn't demonstrate a great deal of natural aptitude, preferred waving his little clubs in the air and pretending to be Fred Flintstone or Barney Rubble than upswinging, downswinging and following through. Jas preferred knocking a football around with the girl from across the road, and untying the ribbons in her hair. At some point fairly early on, Miles abandoned the idea of training up a future winner of the Open.

Golf, however, remained an abiding interest. His conversation was peppered with handicaps and medals, woods, irons and putters, birdies and eagles, fairways, roughs and bunkers. Not to mention the joys of being accepted as a member of the club.

Joining the club isn't just about wanting to hit a ball around, he said, putting a golf ball across the living room carpet into a practice metal hole with articulated sides which flattened to let the ball in, then sprang up again to hold it in place. You have to apply, to be approved, accepted. Somebody has to put your name forward to a committee which checks out your particulars and deliberates on your suitability. Are you their sort of person? Like-minded, of suitable standing, with something to offer?

He hadn't shelled out hard cash for a set of clubs and a leather bag to lug them around, for studded shoes and a giant umbrella for fun, oh no. It was all part of a plan, an investment plan. The golf club was the place to meet the kind of people it was high time he came into contact with, successful people with money to spare and sufficiently discerning taste to consider parting with their cash for art, *his* art in particular. All he had to do was play a lot of golf, repair to the nineteenth hole and bide his time.

If wishes were horses, said Vera.

The club accepted women members and on occasion he tried to persuade his wife to join him on the fairway.

Good for you, Vera. Fresh air and exercise other than gardening. And it has to be said, you've been putting on the beef. An opportunity to shed a few pounds, shape up and meet some new people. You might even pick up a few more piano pupils into the bargain.

As if I don't have enough already.

I'm not saying you have to take on *more* pupils necessarily. You could simply become more *selective*.

Can I afford to be selective, Miles? Can I pick and choose my pupils?

If you made more of the right contacts, the selection would already have been made for you. You could team up with some of the lady golfers. We could play mixed foursomes! You don't get out enough, Vera. You don't see enough of the world.

Hanging around the nineteenth hole with lady golfers and their permanent waves, their smokers' coughs and cultured pearls, is not something I aspire to.

You're behind the times, Vera. Out of touch. These women are forward-thinking, liberal-minded. You could at least give it a try, for my sake. Come along and keep me company, like other men's wives.

Other men's wives, the ones you're talking about, don't work in the evenings. Most of those women don't work at all. They don't have to.

Is that my fault? Are you saying I forced you to take in pupils? Is that what you're saying? It was *your* choice. I could live without the racket they make, hammering the ivories night after night. I could live without it, I tell you.

Are you saying we don't need the money?

I'm *saying* coming to the club with me once in while wouldn't kill you.

He stuck on his golf cap and slung his golf bag over his shoulder. A man afflicted by premature baldness, Gala's father rarely left the house bare-headed. He did not, however, succumb to the artistic affectation of the beret. Perhaps Tony Hancock's impression in *The Rebel* of a hopeless and hapless aspiring artist had put him off. Or perhaps Monsieur Claude, the Onion Johnny, who sported a Gallic beret and striped Breton jersey, had done the trick.

During an earlier period in his life, Miles had worn a beret and worn it proudly. In the old chocolate box, alongside all the other faded old family photos which Vera riffled through when she was feeling sentimental, drawing Gala's attention to this or that long-dead relative she'd never met, was a group portrait of Miles alongside members of an Indian Army tank regiment. Clean-shaven Brits in berets and turbanned, lushly bearded Sikhs. Miles was a young man then, with a bootlace moustache, dark, wavy hair and a smile which showed off his own, short-lived teeth.

He had a trilby for dog walking, a deerstalker with droopy, doglike earflaps for spells of outdoor painting. He had a Dr Zhivago hat for icy weather and a straw Panama for the sun. The charcoal fedora was yet to be purchased.

For the golf course, he quickly acquired a whole range of caps to protect his head from the elements: for sun, lightweight canvas punctured with air holes; for rain, waxed cotton; for cold winds, corduroy or camel hair. Under no circumstances was a specialist garment like a golf cap to be confused with the flat cap or bunnet, traditional head covering of the working man. Nobody who wore a bunnet was likely to be invited to join the club. Some members might have considered a high-end tradesman if he had exceptionally good connections with existing members. But the main point of a club, after all, was to let some in and keep others out.

After piano lessons, Gala had to spend a deal of time waiting in the car, in the golf club car park, listening to her mother tutting at the sight of lady golfers leaving the eighteenth hole and making their way to the clubhouse. The lady golfers wore polo neck jerseys in pastel hues, sharply pressed slacks and spiked shoes with curling tongues. They wore blazers or plain waterproof jackets, pink or coral lipstick and short, styled hair. Altogether they were neat, tidy, smart; members of a club that Gala's mother would never be able to join.

Wedding Belles

ON A CRUMPLED aerogramme which lurked in Gala's bag for
several weeks before being posted:

Dear Mum and Dad,
    I know I said I was just stopping off here for a
couple of weeks but I've decided to stay on. Well, I
already have stayed longer than a couple of weeks,
and now my visa's about to run out so I have to see
whether I can renew it. The money I brought with me
didn't last anything like as long as I'd hoped so it makes
sense to stay where I know people rather than trying
to find work in Mexico where I don't know anybody
and can't speak the language. Language isn't a problem
here though there are more differences than I expected.
People are forever telling me my accent – they call it
my 'brogue' – is cute and complimenting me on how
well I speak English. They seem to think everybody in
Scotland speaks Gaelic! Next week I'm going to a new
place, as Cath has to move house and won't have room
for me.
    It's getting a lot colder. I didn't bring warm enough
clothes. Thought I'd be further south by now and
soaking up the sun. There are charity shops – they call

*them thrift shops – and you can pick up some good
stuff for a few dollars but it's not something people here
do if they can help it. They brag about how much they
paid for something rather than how little!*

*Haven't made much progress with learning Spanish.
It will be easier when I'm hearing it spoken. Still
planning to cross the Rio Grande!*

Love, Gala.

What didn't go in were a few facts which would have sent
her father's blood pressure through the roof, up to high doh,
into a bunker, and possibly brought on another event. Events
were of two types: one related to his heart, the other to his
mind. Her mother would probably, almost certainly should
she have been given the choice, have preferred a heart event.
At least with the heart, she and the doctors knew what was
happening; heart behaviour could be recorded on a monitor,
even if the psychological fallout from a malfunction had not
been greatly researched.

For Gala, things happened very quickly but that's not why
she didn't fill in her parents on her altered, newly married
status. It was more to do with the fact that her husband
was gay, black and worked the tables of the bar above the
apartment she subsequently rented. The apartment was cheap,
noisy from the bar, barely furnished. Platoons of cockroaches
bigger than pecans lived beneath the bed, alongside a stack of
gay porn left by a previous tenant. Her legal husband had his
own, sparkling apartment on the other side of the bar. Some
nights his boyfriend stayed over, some he slept alone and some
he showed a new kid in town a good time.

The marriage had been rash, impulsive, a flurry of snap
decisions culminating in the mother of all parties: cute guys
and confetti everywhere, Gloria Gaynor on replay.

Relegation of the Wheel

POTTERY BEGAN TO lose its attraction for Gala's father. Disasters with glazes, poor functionality – the fruit bowls were cumbersome, the teapots inefficient – took the edge off his enthusiasm. He was fed up with lugging sacks of sweaty clay around – *Aaagh, Lumbago*! he'd cry, *Lumbago*! as if he were summoning up some bright island with parrots and palm trees, women in clothes the colours of roses and slim, cinnamon-skinned men with astonishing smiles; where noon was white heat and darkness aswarm with the hiss and scritch of the jungle, the prayer bells of monks. But no, lumbago was just boring old backache.

Sales of his terracotta and stoneware creations had been disappointing. A person could find a use for only so many fruit bowls and teapots and after Miles had persuaded her mother's friends and his own friends' wives, and these two groups were on the way to becoming mutually exclusive, to purchase one or two for themselves and, if possible, an additional one or two as gifts, the outlets dried up.

All those connections, those overlapping groups, interlocking circles he'd hoped to tap into for his pyramid selling of *Swipe!* – what had become of them? They existed, he was sure. If only he could get the word around all those contacts of contacts that here, on their heavily mortgaged suburban doorstep, was some first-rate, hand-thrown artwork at a very affordable price, ceramics which were not only aesthetically pleasing but also functional, if not quite as functional as the factory-made variety. Had someone put a spanner in the works to prevent him access to the magical chain link? And if so, who might that have been? Some other local potter who didn't take kindly to a bit of healthy competition? Someone had it in for him, someone was blackballing him. That was it; that was the only explanation.

Fruit bowls and teapots in grey brown, grey blue, grey yellow, grey white – dirty colours to Gala, subtle, subtle! to her father – lined the studio shelves and were stacked like chimneypots in the back of the garage. Even with the additional shelving he'd added to the sitting room, the hall and living room, his wood carvings, bronze heads and figurines took over every available nook, alcove and shelf. Vera complained about the amount of dusting, not that she ever did much dusting. And Gran, who did, incorporated each *objet d'art* into her chores without a hint of complaint.

For everyday use, Gran stuck with a reliable old stainless steel teapot, which poured like a dream and could be thoroughly scrubbed free of tannin spots. When Miles and Vera had visitors, however, she loyally set out the hand-thrown mugs, laid biscuits on a drab, hand-thrown plate, after adding a paper doily to brighten it up, and brewed up in a hand-thrown stoneware teapot. The teapot poured in stops and starts, like a blocked pipe, but Gran would always blame any spills on herself:

Dear, dear, I'm such a silly old butterfingers.

She had a steadier hand than Miles.

To get anywhere with pottery, Vera suggested, Miles would have to make his ceramics more innovative and sophisticated. Perhaps he might take lessons from someone with more experience in the field?

Me, take lessons?

What about producing more cheap and cheerful items, then, things people can actually *use* on an everyday basis?

Any old jobbing potter can do donkey work like that, he replied. I'm not cut out for that. I'm an artist!

One night, after a good deal of pacing, smoking and slugging at the Dimple, after Marlene falling in love again and again and doing all the other things she was so good at, he shoved the kick-wheel into a corner and covered it with a dustsheet. Under the skylight, in privileged position, the easel, the palette, the tubes of oils and jars of paintbrushes were reinstated.

Galaxy

GALA HADN'T WANTED to enter the competition. It had been her mother's decision, after consultation with Mrs Hammond. On this, Miles supported Vera. No point in spending good money unless there's something to show for it. Since she started lessons, Gala had been sitting a piano exam a year. Jas had also been sent to lessons but as he showed less aptitude for scales and arpeggios, ear tests and sight reading, and demonstrated less likelihood of coming out of an exam with flying colours, his lessons were terminated. No point in spending good money etc. etc., but then again, as Miles continued, passing an exam didn't bring much recognition, and where were you without recognition?

Mrs Hammond was nice enough and spent less time trilling along to the tune and dotting in and out of the music room than her mother did. She was patient but particular and knew straight away if Gala had been slacking. Not that skipping practice was easy for the daughter of a piano teacher; Vera might have been taken up with her own studies but still, regular as a metronome, *practice* would interrupt Vera's train of thought and Gala would be sent off, again, to confront the set pieces.

The first was a Beethoven prelude. After a while it became satisfying to play: it wasn't too fast and didn't have too many accidentals or changes of time signature. The second, 'Month's Mind', by John Ireland, was slow, mournful and modern, with odd-sounding chords, tricky rhythms and big stretches. The title had something to with the past and the dead. Mrs Hammond didn't seem to know exactly what, and neither did her mother. The mood was slippery. It wasn't full-blown grief, more of a reaching towards something or somebody you could never grasp hold of. Sometimes Gala thought she'd caught it. Other times she knew she was way off. She practised the Beethoven and the Ireland until they were trapped in her head, if not entirely secure in her fingertips.

Her father dropped her off at the venue and went on to work. Her mother had an application deadline to meet. The absence of both parents was a good thing: in the event of a complete disaster, there would be no key witnesses, no first-hand evidence to hold against her. Gala wouldn't have minded Jas or Gran going along with her but Jas was at school and Gran had a bad chest.

The competition had two stages. Everybody would play the Beethoven. The adjudicators would confer. Only one out of three would go through to the second round and play the Ireland. The crush in the waiting room was awful: the boasting, the bravado, the squawks and guffaws, the smells of crisps and licorice and pre-pubescent body odour. Gala didn't know anybody. Most of the contestants were from boarding or private schools; she could tell by the uniforms, and the clear-skinned complexions.

A trim, prim woman in a pleated skirt stood at the door and called out names:

Rosemary Symington! This way please. *Marjorie Frick.* Hurry along now.

Gala's fingers dripped sweat. If she couldn't get them to dry up, they'd slither all over the keys. Wiping her hands on her blazer didn't help at all but then she remembered: Gran had wrapped a small bottle of eau de cologne in a hanky and stuck it in her pocket.

That'll see ye right. And here, Gran had said, slipping her a half crown. For luck.

She soaked the hanky in cologne and wiped her hands thoroughly: fingers, palms, lifelines, lovelines, nails, cuticles. She was sweating around the hairline too, on the upper lip and behind the ears but there was only enough cologne to take care of her hands.

Suddenly somebody shoved up against her and nearly knocked her flying.

Sorry. Terribly sorry. Domino effect. Bloke down by the door bumped the next man and so on down the line. We're like sardines in here. Domino sardines, hah! The new party game. And the winner is – ! You look like a wet weekend.

He was a dark-eyed boy with a soft mouth and nice teeth.

I hate competitions, said Gala.

Could be worse. Got us out of school for a day. I'm Lenny. How d'you do.

He extricated his arm from the scrum of bodies, held out his long, elegant hand. A pianist's hand.

Where's your music?

Didn't bring it. Playing by ear. The parentals promised that if I'm placed, they'll buy me a new bike!

Catriona McKirtle. Teresa Finnegan. Leonard Trockel.

That's me. Old cow's got some timing! So what's your name?

Gala.

Gala? As in Bunting?

Don't be stupid! You don't have to play by ear, do you? Nobody said –

Nah. Playing by ear is not *obligatory*. But it is *permissible*. And might impress the judges.

Leonard Trockel. Immediately!

Wish me luck!

Good luck!

Same to you when your turn comes. S'cuse me folks! Make way now! You're delaying a future virtuoso. These fingers are worth their weight in gold medals!

Bright-eyed, empty-handed, Lenny elbowed his way to the corridor, accompanied by smirks and giggles.

When Gala's turn came, she clomped onto the creaking

stage, sat at the Steinway grand, ventured a glance at the massive auditorium and the sparse audience. A few overdressed mothers were scattered around, a few lone fathers, ill at ease on the wooden chairs, some plumped and expectant grannies and great aunts, a tight knot of adjudicators. She began. She continued. She was finished before she knew it. As instructed, she stood up, bowed stiffly and left the stage.

No bum notes, no actual mistakes but of course that in itself is never enough. You had to get the expression right, the *tempi,* the phrasing.

Hey, Bunting! How'd it go?

It was Lenny, looking very pink.

Okay, I think. Can't really tell. It just whizzed by. You?

Total cock-up. Blanked half way through. Totally. Got going again after what seemed like forever but what a bleeding cock-up! Bang goes the bike.

He was smiling hard but his eyes were teary.

You were brave to try, said Gala. I'd never have risked it.

Just showing off as usual. Serves me right. Listen, if there's a God in heaven and I do get through to the second round, could I borrow your music?

Yeah, she said. Any time.

No, no – just this once. Cross my heart, hope to die and be chopped up into little pieces and fed to pigs which will band together and throw themselves off a cliff –

The administrator returned, tapped a ruler against the door for silence then read out the list of those who had made it through to the second round. Gala's name was on the list. Lenny's wasn't. At that point most of the rejects buttoned their blazers, buckled up their music satchels and made a beeline for the door; they couldn't wait to get shot of the place, to cool their burning cheeks, their shame and disappointment in the soothing anonymity of city streets.

I'll wait, said Lenny, as Gala was instructed to make her way to the auditorium. See how you do.

You don't have to, she said. I'll probably make a... a cock-up of it. She'd never even heard the expression before that day, far less used it. But she knew it was rude. And thrilling.

Gala was awarded first prize in her category. After the results were announced, winners duly applauded and certificates handed out, a few contestants congratulated Gala. As none of the other contestants had heard any performance but their own, how could they tell whether she deserved to win or whether the adjudicators had got it all wrong? Lenny was sprawled out, feet up on the bench, watching with some amusement what was, once again, a rapid exodus.

Young man, said the administrator, please remove your footwear from the seating area. You do see the sign, don't you? I take it you can read?

Lenny mooed at her. She humphed and sighed, plucked a crisp packet from the floor between two sharply filed fingernails then stalked off down the corridor. Gala slipped her certificate between the Beethoven and the Ireland and buttoned up her blazer. She and Lenny were the last two in the waiting room. After the previous crush and bustle, the drab, stale space became suddenly intimate, personal.

Here, said Lenny, handing her a slightly melted bar of chocolate. Your prize from me.

Galaxy! said Gala. My favourite! Better than a stupid certificate.

Too right. All that slog for a bit of paper and a pat on the back. Will you come back next year?

Hope not. Will you?

No choice, m'dear. The parentals. Need to see me compete. At any cost.

Bring your music next time.

Mind-reader as well as prize-winner? Well, I'm offski. To face the plinking music. So long, farewell, auf weidersehen, goodnight. I hate to go and leave this bloody awful sight –

Lenny leaned over, kissed her on the cheek then strode off, hands in pockets, without a backwards glance.

Gala's father was teaching late so she was taking the train home. It was only a short walk to the station. The platform was sunny, the sky blue with fluffy white clouds. After a few minutes, the train arrived. The compartment was deserted. Gala put her feet up on the seat, something she'd never before dared to do, unwrapped the chocolate bar and consumed it slowly, lingering over each mouthful, chocolatey fingertips stroking the cheek which Lenny had kissed.

At home, over the evening meal, her mother repeated the adjudicator's note which accompanied her certificate several times: *an almost flawless performance, touched with sensitivity.* Did her mother stress the word 'almost' or is that just how she remembers it? Gala told about how Gran's eau de cologne had come to the rescue, about how noisy and busy the waiting room had been, how Lenny had bravely tried to play by ear, how funny he was, how nice he'd been to her. She didn't, of course, use the word 'cock-up'. She mentioned the chocolate bar but not the kiss. Gran said that pride goes before a fall but a good spirit is priceless. Jas said nothing. Her mother said that coming a cropper would teach him a lesson. Her father concurred and, after mulling over the name, wanted to know whether Lenny was Jewish. Gala thought: How the hell would she know and what the hell did it matter? Gala said that she didn't know. Years later, she heard that Lenny had become a concert pianist. She never saw him again.

Figuratively Speaking

IT BEGAN TO dawn on Gala that other people's parents sometimes went out together because they enjoyed each other's company. The Douglases next door were always off somewhere, Mr Douglas holding the door of his glossy car for his glossy wife in her fur coat and high heels. Mr and Mrs Billings, the parents of Gala's friend Mags, one door down from the Douglases, went out together every Saturday night.

Mr Douglas sold cars. Mrs Douglas threw lots of parties. Mr Billings had a factory which made stapling machines and Mrs Billings cooked tasty meals and cleaned industriously for a family of seven. There was always enough food for Gala to stay for tea at short notice. Mr Billings would come home from his factory, kiss his wife on the cheek and announce that he had tickets for *From Russia with Love*, *Goldfinger*, or a cabaret at The Pavilion, or that he'd booked a table at the Steak House. Every time, as if her husband had never surprised her before in this manner, Mrs Billings would break into a delighted smile, remove her pinny and hurry off to doll herself up.

Gala's mother claimed she was too busy for such indulgent entertainment. As well as giving piano lessons several evenings a week, she had embarked on a teacher training course and spent pupil-free evenings studying in her bedroom or wandering about the house, quoting aloud her current essay questions:

Does Willy Loman's behaviour in *Death of a Salesman* *affect* his family or *infect* it? In *The Birthday Party*, how is the central theme of isolation developed and resolved according to contemporary behavioural theory? In *King Lear*, do Goneril and Regan epitomise evil incarnate or have they been misunderstood in the context of Lear's relationship with Cordelia?

Was her mother hoping to pluck some inspiration from the air? Nobody in the house was in a position to make any useful suggestions.

Gala doesn't remember her parents going out as a couple but a small, framed photo in the living room alcove showed them – when Vera was slim and almost stylish – with Lou and Beattie McCord. An indoor shot, taken with a flash, showed the two couples flushed and merry – and in party hats – saying *cheese* in a night club. A night club! A place which played jazz and swing, where people danced! She'd never seen her parents dance. Not even at Christmas or New Year. Or hold hands. Or kiss, other than a brisk *hello* or *goodbye* peck on the cheek.

One autumn night a sniping sort of conversation had been going, off and on, whenever her parents crossed paths in the living room, her mother emerging from studying in the bedroom, her father coming in from the studio to resume his attempts at persuasion.

So you won't come?

You know it's not my sort of thing.

But it's *my* sort of thing. And I'm your *husband*. You should support me. That's what a wife is meant to do.

I don't see why supporting you has to involve traipsing along to The Alhambra to hear some old has-been.

She's a world-class performer, for heaven's sake. Playing to packed houses here, there and everywhere. She's a phenomenon.

In Berlin, they told her to get lost. To go back to America. Her own people thought she'd betrayed them.

That's all water under the bridge. This is a chance in a lifetime to see her in the flesh.

I'd prefer to give that a miss.

I was speaking *figuratively*, Vera. Don't you have a grasp of figurative language? You spend hour upon hour reading plays and the like but you take everything so *literally*.

Parading around in fishnets and frilly pants.

She was playing a part, Vera. A *role*. *The Blue Angel*, now that was a film. *Shanghai Express, The Devil is a Woman* –

Frilly pants or a top hat and tails.

Yes. I found that look rather fetching.

If you ask me, she's just a jumped-up trollop who got her big break on the casting couch.

Even if she did, all that must be behind her now. But her singing is timeless. Timeless. She'll be elegant, sophisticated. In a floor-length gown.

Slit to her thigh.

These are modern times, Vera. D'you know what I think? I think you're jealous. The woman must be sixty-five if she's a day and still looks like the belle of the ball. Whereas you look like a frump. You are a frump. And a prude. What did I do to deserve a frump and a prude? I'll see if one of the chaps at the club is interested. Or go alone, if need be. I deserve a treat. Get precious little in that department at home.

Perspective

WHILE THE UNUSED sprayguns of *Swipe!* gathered dust, his enthusiasm for Diversion waned and the commissions for church fonts and garden sculpture dried up, Gala's father began to reconsider himself as a painter and once again was in caged bear mode: pacing, smoking, talking up his painterly talents before he'd got around to stretching any canvases. The theory was that if he said he was going to do a thing, he would.

I see things through, he said. I've got backbone. I'm no quitter.

Once again he was convinced he'd hit on a great idea. Why hadn't he thought of it before? He'd let himself become sidetracked by other projects but that was in the past. This time he'd crack it. Painting was what he should have been doing all along. Painting was his true vocation and there was no time like the present.

He decided to begin with landscapes.

Easier to deal with than people, he said. Landscapes don't talk back. Don't let you down.

On the first dry Sunday he packed the boot with a portable easel, paints, palette and folding chair, herded the family into the car and hit the road for Loch Lomond. From where the Price family lived, on the green hem of the city, it was open road all the way. No speed limit, no traffic lights, no diversions. On family outings it was always Miles behind the wheel, putting the foot down, careering round blind bends, slamming on the brakes and cursing. And Vera urging him to slow down, to heed the speed limit, hazard warnings and all the other idiots on the road.

Father ignored mother. Mother persisted in offering advice. Gala, Gran and Jas slid around the back seat, crackling sweetie papers and clutching their bellies as the scenery jolted and blurred.

A good driver can take a calculated risk, said Miles. With my driving experience I don't have to stay stuck behind some slowcoach who's hogging the road.

He wasn't a good driver. Only a lucky one. When something of interest caught his eye, he'd stop, bump the car onto the grass verge and tramp down to the lochside for a closer look. He'd raise a hand to his brow, narrow his eyes and scan the area like a hawk in search of a mouse to pounce on. If, on further inspection, something wasn't right about the location, the foreground, background, *chiaroscuro*, composition, he would drive on doggedly, stop somewhere else and repeat the process while the rest of the family waited in the car, hot and sticky and bored.

He was always on the lookout for a better location, always had a hunch that one lay just around the next bend on the narrow, winding road, so on they went, only to discover that there wasn't even a place to pull in, never mind offer access to the lochside.

At one point he made a U-turn, narrowly avoiding getting stuck in a ditch, drove back to a spot where he'd previously stopped for a second look, decided, after all, that he was right to reject it the first time, and made a second U-turn. Vera issued dire warnings about trucks piled high with timber or sheep hurtling round the bend and making mincemeat of them all.

Eventually, his eye caught by a ray of sunlight glancing through the quivering, gilded leaves of a stand of silver birch – he was inordinately fond of silver birch – he pulled up sharply and switched off the engine.

This'll have to do.

The family trundled after their leader. Everyone was under orders to amuse themselves while he did some charcoal sketches and watercolour washes. He preferred cloudy days. Better tonality, he said. Elsewhere on the lochside were plenty places to paddle, to kick a ball or stretch out on sandy banks amid sweet grass, wildflowers and the twittering of small, quick birds, but the vistas Gala's father found topographically appealing could, it seemed, only be observed from scraps of rocky shoreline surrounded by bog.

Gran and Vera sought out boulders to perch on. They spread travelling rugs over lumps and bumps, shared a flask of tea and gazed out on the grey loch. Jas skiffed stones and tried, unsuccessfully, to bounce a ball on the shingle beach, until he was told that the racket he was making was disturbing his father's concentration. Gala also tried a spot of painting, but the breeze slapped the paper about and the water pot, which her father grudgingly provided, was forever toppling over. With his portable easel, his clips and drawing board, her father was patently much better equipped for painting *al fresco*.

Coarse grasses, rusty bulrushes and brackish water appealed to him. Dirty colours. And thin, squint trees against a background of slate blue hills. In case he didn't approve of his daughter copying his ideas, Gala would have chosen another subject but as he had decided on the spot precisely for that particular combination, there was little else to look at.

That's lovely dear, Gran said of Gala's attempt. Much better than I could dae in a month o Sundays.

Jas wandered over, had a look, and said nothing. He had no desire to replicate the unexciting world around him and as he had been banned from doing what came naturally, was at a loss as to how to pass the time.

Watch you don't spill that dirty paint water on your clean shorts, said her mother.

Gala's painting was messy and drippy but the bulrushes weren't bad. Mixing the exact turdy brown, somewhere between burnt umber and raw sienna, hadn't been easy but she felt it was a reasonably dirty approximation. She wasn't so sure about the miserable colour of the grasses – not quite Brasso yellow, not quite mustard.

You've got the perspective all wrong, said her father. It's like a Chinese painting. The Chinese knew a good deal about watercolours and ink drawing, I'll give them that, but not a lot about perspective.

Nothing Like Family

INSIDE A BIRTHDAY card, a reproduction of one of her father's landscapes, stapled to an International Money Order:

Dear Gala,
    It was a bit of a dreary Christmas without you here, although Beattie McCord and some of her brood came over on Boxing Day which brightened things up a bit, in spite of her loss. Poor Beattie has been through the mill. First Lou – did I tell you Lou died? Out of the blue. No warning at all. One day he was right as rain, the next he was in the throes of a massive stroke which did for him. And then a few months later, again completely out of the blue, Mrs Wellsley passed away, with her embroidery needle still in her hand. Which just goes to show you never know the moment. I don't think Beattie's really got over the grief but she does have her family around her, which must be a great support. There's nothing like family when the chips are down.
    Well, have a good birthday and buy yourself something nice. We miss you and hope you get the travel bug out of your system soon.
    Mum xxx

Swansdown and Diamante

A NIGHT IN November. Cold. Wet. Shiny pavements. A seethe of starlings. Miles was off to The Alhambra, via a quick pre-show snifter with Johnny Brock, an often-cited but rarely seen acquaintance. On the drive to town, he'd been as fidgety as a boy on a first date, checking his appearance in the rearview mirror, tipping his new hat – a charcoal fedora – this way and that, adjusting the knot on his garish kipper tie, straightening his collar, patting the breast pocket of his corduroy jacket, checking far too often that he had his ticket.

Gala and Gran were going to the ballet at The King's: Gran's treat; Gala had done well in her ballet exam. As they crossed the road, leaning into the driving rain, Gran slithered on the wet cobbles, lost her balance, and clutched Gala's arm.

Dearie me, she said, righting herself. Near a goner there. Skiting aboot like a clown. Is this us?

Must be. There's the prima ballerina.

Gran scanned the street.

Whereaboots?

On the poster!

Aye, aye, right ye are.

The prima ballerina couldn't be on the street right now, Gran. She'd have to be in her dressing room, doing her make-up.

Silly old me. But she's lovely, isn't she? Lovely.

They joined the queue outside the theatre. Umbrellas lined the building like a border of black, densely packed shrubs. Orange lightbulbs picked out the words The King's Theatre and reflections thrown back by shiny pavements gave a warm glow to the pallid faces of those in the queue. A man with an accordion approached. His face was red raw, his clothes soaked through. From his battered instrument, he squeezed out a harsh bleating, like a sheep caught on barbed wire. Gran greeted him with her warmest smile.

Now that's a bonny tune, son. Where have I heard that afore? To Gala she whispered: Look in ma handbag, dear. Can you see ma purse?

The man was skinny as a whippet. The smell which came off him was like a sour shield. His fingers fumbled and slithered over the keys, hitting wrong notes galore. It was hard to tell how the tune was meant to sound or if he was even playing a tune at all; he might as well have been making it up as he went along. He didn't say anything, just kept squeezing away, standing directly in front of Gala, looking straight through her as if she were made of glass.

Gie the fella a shillin, dear, said Gran. I'm sure there's a shillin in ma purse. He'll mibbe hae a family tae feed. If no, he'll hae plenty ither ways tae part wi it.

A shilling, Gala thought, was a lot to hand over on account of such an awful racket.

Gie the fella a shillin, dear.

Reluctantly, Gala held out the coin. The man's hand flew off his instrument, snatched the coin and slipped it into his waistcoat pocket, with the speed and sleight of Artful Arcady performing one of his card tricks. He gave the barest of nods, so minimal it might just have been a twitch, then moved off down the queue.

They were way up in the gods, close to the ceiling where plaster cherubs, with mischievous amusement, surveyed the audience. The seats were so high up and the rows so steeply raked that

Gala felt her centre of gravity shift, tilt, as if at the slightest knock she might topple over the rail, roll and bounce across the Grand Circle, flip over its ornate rail and thud into the stalls, bruised and battered and possibly dead.

Gran passed over a bag of sweeties. The house lights dipped and the tilting subsided.

Take a couple the now so we dinny crackle once the show's on the go.

The first half was extracts from *Swan Lake* and *Giselle*. Ballerinas in feathery tutus with shapely legs and flat chests picked about on *pointes*, hair scraped back and covered with feather caps or set off by tiaras. The male dancers, in white tights, displayed bulging thighs and groins. They strode, or leapt, or supported ballerinas in arabesques and pirouettes. It was all graceful and shapely. The music was sad and passionate. After a while, though Gala still clung to remnants of the 'When I grow up I want to be a ballerina' fantasy, she became just a little bored. The moves were repetitive, the acting hammy. The men, in the poses they struck, looked unlike any men she'd ever seen, the arrow clearly didn't pierce the swan princess's heart and she collapsed far too elegantly for somebody who had been mortally wounded.

After the interval, during which she and Gran licked vanilla ice cream off flat little wooden spoons then took turns to use the programme as a fan, the curtain rose once more on a stage flooded with red light. The set was a cocktail bar. Women in slinky red dresses lounged around on high stools or leaned against pillars, rearranging their limbs, smoking cigarettes and drinking from long-stemmed, wide-brimmed glasses. Red, black, and the pinkish white which went by the name *flesh-coloured* featured extensively. Not all the flesh-coloured areas were an illusion created by body-stockings and tights: some of them, quite a lot in fact, were bare skin.

I think we're in some sorta bordello! Gran whispered. Wi women o ill repute!

The music was smoky and jazzy. The female dancers did a lot of close, slithery moves with each other and with the men. Nobody was on *pointes*. No arabesques or pirouettes were executed with consummate skill. There was no pining for absent lovers, no tragic but unconvincing deaths. There were, however, a number of jealous lovers and rough, almost realistic fighting.

The atmosphere was tense. At one point a man grabbed one of the women and tried to kiss her. She pushed him away. He grabbed her again, roughly, pushing her head back and yanking her by the hair. She struggled, he grabbed her again. This time he tore at her dress, ripped it right off. The woman acted upset but didn't do anything to cover herself up and she wasn't even wearing a bra. She was topless! And stayed topless right up to the final curtain.

Dearie me, said Gran with a quavery giggle as they joined the exodus stepping down the eternal, winding staircase from the gods, that wis a bit racy!

The rain beat on the car roof. Gala's father, fedora at a rakish angle, gripped the steering wheel with both hands, peered through the streaming windscreen at the hazy road ahead.

Marvellous! he said. Bloody marvellous!

You got yir money's worth, then? said Gran.

You can say that again. Three encores. Three! Worth every penny. *Outside the barracks, in the pouring rain* – I'd happily sit through it all over again – *Falling in love again, never wanted to, what am I to do, I can't help it.*

My word, said Gran. Ye'd better no let Vera hear that. She'll fair take the hump.

Might make her pull her socks up. Sorry, Lottie. Forget I said that. Mum's the word, eh? Bloody hell!

He swerved just in time to avoid a parked car.

Of all the stupid places to park! Impossible to see, especially in this weather – *I'm warm again, my pack is light, it's you, Lili Marleen, it's you Lili Marleen.*

I like that yin, said Gran. Catchy. But sad, tae. Reminds me o the Blitz.

A night to remember! A once-in-a-lifetime experience!

His voice outdid the rain.

And did Johnny Brock enjoy the show?

Oh yes. I'd say every full-blooded man in the audience enjoyed the show immensely. More men than women in the audience, you know. And some of the women were – he lowered his voice – the *short back and sides* variety. In *trouser suits*!

Dearie me, said Gran.

And between you and me – he lowered his voice again and of course Gala listened more closely – there was a rather sizeable contingent of *nancy boys*, swanking around, brazen as all come out.

Marlene's aye been popular wi aw sorts, said Gran.

Don't know what the world's coming to when that sort can go parading around, happy as Larry.

They're aw God's children. Anybody for a chocolate raisin? said Gran, rustling her poke of sweeties.

Too much *licence* these days, too much *libertarianism,* he continued. We should never have done away with National Service.

Och, dinny let ony o that spoil yir night, Miles.

A good dose of discipline would knock those limp-wristed jessies into shape.

So whit were the great lady's costumes like? Did Marlene wear lovely dresses?

Gowns. Gorgeous gowns. The acme of glamour. Diamante from top to toe. Marvellous. And that swansdown cloak has to be seen to be believed. And how was the ballet?

Lovely, said Gran. We had a grand time, didn't we?

It was great. We were so high up we could almost touch the angels on the ceiling.

I don't have much time for ballet, myself, said Miles. Men in tights prancing around.

They were only in tights for the first bit, said Gala. After that the men wore proper trousers.

Good thing too, if you ask me. Men in tights! Leaves no room for the imagination.

The rain streamed down the windscreen. The wipers clicked

back and forth at top speed but were having little effect. Street lights were a fuzz of yellow, traffic lights a smear of green, amber, red.

Falling in love again, her father sang, *never wanted to, what am I to do, I caaaaan't help it.*

Deconstruction of a Turban

MILES WAS UP a ladder, Panama hat protecting his bald head. He was trimming the top of the hedge. It was a close afternoon, with the dusty sweetness of blown roses in the air. Overhead, clouds were stacking up into thunderheads. Gala was bored. It was a Saturday. The few friends she'd made since she changed school all lived on the other side of the city. You couldn't just show up at the door, you had to be invited. The friends she'd had in primary dropped her the minute they found out that she was being sent to a private school in the city, as if she'd developed body odour.

Even Mags, who'd sworn blind it wouldn't make any difference that she wasn't going to the same school, became unaccountably busy when she called round: she had homework to do, which she'd never given two hoots about before; she had to help her mother, who'd never needed her help before; she had to go out somewhere unspecific at that very moment; she had promised to meet another girl, whom she'd never liked before, at the youth club, which she'd never liked before.

It made no difference that Gala begged her parents not to be sent to the gloomy old dump with the dreary uniform and a headmistress who looked like Queen Victoria in mourning. Her parents, as always, claimed they knew best. Well they didn't. She'd been there a year, and though she might have got used to it, and though some of the girls were okay, she'd never like it.

If she didn't find something to do, her father would rope her into some gardening. She'd sew something, that's what she'd do. A dress, maybe. At primary school she had acquired some basic sewing skills by way of dull, painstaking labour on articles which nobody was ever likely to use. The worst and most pointless task of all had been to hand-stitch a pair of seersucker knickers. When you could buy ready-made figure-hugging bri-nylon hipster briefs in a six different colours, what modern girl was ever going to wear puffy-out, old-lady bloomers? All the practice from the knickers, and before them the lapbag, the dishcloths and the table runner, however, meant that she could produce a reasonably uniform running stitch.

The Price household wasn't big on sewing. Gran could do basic repairs but was beginning to have trouble with anything fiddly. *Handless*, she'd say. *I'm handless*, which wasn't true but she did struggle to thread a needle. She'd persevere, but it grieved her when she made a mess of something. As for Gala's mother, Vera could, at a pinch, sew on a button or darn a sock but had little inclination to do either. As a result, the remnant box was more of a ragbag than a treasure trove. Other people, whose mothers sewed, had swathes of glinting taffeta and slippery satin, of wispy chiffon and plush velvet. Other people had a host of haberdashery: sequinned ribbons, trims of lace, and fur. Having little to work with other than faded damask tablecloths and ripped curtains, Gala coveted other people's remnant boxes. But she had an idea.

In the kitchen, Gran was chopping onions and weeping.

Remember that sari from Aunt Angela?

Dearie me. Ma tears'll be saltin the soup at this rate.

And the turban?

Haud on till I can see what I'm daein.

She put down her knife, took off her glasses and dabbed her streaming eyes with a corner of her apron.

That's better. You're efter the sari, are ye?

And the turban.

After a lengthy rummage in the kitchen cabinet, at the very

back of the bottom drawer, both items turned up inside some spotted, discoloured cellophane.

Seek and ye shall find. Mind and check wi your faither afore ye go tamperin wi yon. You never know, he'll mibbe hae some attachment tae them.

Gran bent to shut the drawer. Her scalp showed pink through her thin hair. Would she soon have to wear a wig like Auntie Win?

The grass was dry and warm. Gala unrolled the sari and spread it out. It ran the length of the lawn, like a decorative pathway, its intricate, repeating pattern more like a mosaic than crazy paving.

Look at how long this sari is!

It'll be six yards, her father replied, without turning round. Standard measure.

Can I use it for sewing?

Feel free.

I might have to cut it up.

Be my guest. I thought your mother had turfed it out years ago.

He resumed clipping the hedge. The bees seemed to like the sari. So did the butterflies, which fluttered and settled, fluttered and settled. She held up the turban. A dusty, spicy smell, like Christmas biscuits and old candles, still clung to the waxy fabric.

A turban is also constructed from a single length of cloth, her father continued. Very simple idea. Clever, if primitive. Wind it round and round, pop a fancy pin on the front and hey presto! – an Indian prince.

Too big for her head, the turban slipped down over Gala's nose. She tried to imagine the hot, bright place it had come from, where spice trees spread their scented branches and dangerous animals roamed the jungle.

Is it okay if I unwind the turban?

Please yourself, he said, clipping away. Can't see why Angela sent it on in the first place. As if I'd have any use for a turban.

He tipped the brim of his Panama, rested the shears on the hedge, sat on the top step of the ladder and lit up.

Gala dug her thumbs into the folds of the turban, found an end of the cloth and began to work it free. The end hadn't even been knotted or pinned in position, just wound back on itself and tucked inside. Layer by layer, the turban shrank from being a sturdy nest for a head to a long, thin twist of cloth. Between the windings, sheets of newspaper had been packed to give more body. They were yellowed and brittle. On one sheet was a faded photo of an immense black cloud above a body of water. Otherwise it was covered with columns of curly text in an alphabet she couldn't even begin to read; all she could decipher was the date: 20.12.27.

Dad?

What?

Were you born in 1927?

That's correct. Why?

Because the newspaper inside the sari was printed on the day you were born!

Was it now, he said, flatly. Well, well.

Isn't that amazing! Twenty-ninth of December, 1927.

I don't need to be told my own date of birth.

But don't you think it's a coincidence?

It's no coincidence at all. While I was being born in the middle of England, dragged out of the womb into the sleepy hollow of Toombe, my father was amusing himself in Javanese bazaars. And in the Indian Ocean, baby Krakatoa was causing havoc. So you see, I was born on the same day as a volcano erupted. He hacked away at the hedge for a bit longer, clumped down the ladder, tossed the shears onto a heap of springy privet clippings, lit up again and went inside to make himself yet another cup of coffee.

Gala collected up the fragments of tea-coloured newsprint. They were frail and crumbly, as if they might turn to dust at any moment. The sun was getting hotter and dark clouds were piling up even higher. The air crackled and throbbed. Carefully Gala slipped the scraps of newsprint inside an old pillowcase and slid it to the bottom of the remnant box. The undone turban lay on the grass like a sloughed snakeskin, cast off and useless.

She had made it useless. She smoothed out the creases and tried to rewind it, restore it to how it had been before her meddling fingers reduced it to an insignificant strip of cloth, tried and failed until the rain started, big spattering drops falling on the interlocking patterns of a sari which stretched the length of the lawn, and a spoiled turban, as old as her father.

The Art of Sitting

NOW THAT HE was rubbing golf jersey shoulders with people who had some disposable cash lying around, not to mention a healthy self-regard, her father began to see another opportunity. Landscape painting had engendered one or two sales but not as many, not nearly as many as he had hoped. Privately, very privately, Gala thought this might have something to do with his preference for muddy colours.

The people her father intended to target, who had a taste for malt whisky and Havana cigars might, he reckoned, be persuaded to fork out for a portrait of a wife or child. The gleam was back in his eye. Portraits were what people wanted and a portrait in oils was just the ticket, classy and lasting. Watercolours were all very well but didn't command the same respect as oils. Or the same fee.

Once more the studio smelled of turps and linseed. Paint tubes lay scattered on worktops alongside heaps of soggy rags. Brushes rubbed along together in jars of sludge. Canvases were stretched and stacked against the wall in readiness for a string of commissions. Marlene, turned up a notch, put in overtime, crooning throaty seduction.

He had to get his hand in again. And his patience. Oils couldn't be rushed. To build up a depth of colour, each layer had to be laid down and left to dry before the next could be applied.

He had persistence: he could chip away at a chunk of stone or wood for months on end but had precious little patience with paint. In an attempt to achieve maximum productivity – and have some samples to flash around – he embarked on a simultaneous series of family portraits.

Time and motion. Efficiency. Killing two birds with one... canvas!

Gala, Jas and Vera were called upon to sit. Her mother complained before, during and after the sitting. She didn't like the older version of herself which her husband was consigning to canvas. He had a perfectly good portrait of her which he'd done when he was young and in love, which showed off her classic profile to advantage and flattered her in ways which his renewed attempt to capture her essence failed to do. He didn't appreciate the new critical awareness which her teaching training course had fostered, not one bit. He was the artist, she was the sitter. End of story, as far as he was concerned. She should keep her critiques for Shakespeare and Arthur Miller and the like. He did a nice portrait of Jas, in spite of his complaints about Jas's fidgeting and empty-headed expression. Gran was not required. Gran could sit still, emanating warmth, patience and generosity better than anyone but was – though this of course was never said – too old, too wrinkled, too homespun, out of keeping with the calibre of customer Miles hoped to attract.

It was summer. The days were long and scented.

Sit still!

The spars of the chair dug into Gala's spine. Her bum was numb. Her head itched. A fly buzzed into her ear then waded through the sweat at her hairline. She shook her head, flapped it away. To help pass the time she counted all the pictures on the walls. Thirty-three. Then she counted the dirty coffee mugs, five, the whisky glasses, four. Her mother was always complaining about the lack of mugs and glasses in the kitchen cabinet but it never occurred to her to just go out and fetch them from the studio. She'd rather moan than solve the problem. But then why couldn't her father just take his cups back by himself?

These days he was always in and out of the kitchen, making himself coffee, even when Gran was peeling potatoes or taking chicken off the bone, he had to have access to the kettle, the cupboards and the fridge if and when he wanted, no matter what anybody else was doing.

Sit still, I said!

The fumes from the turps were making her feel light-headed. On the walls were two portraits of Gala, pastel drawings, done when she was little, three or four at the most. Too young to sit still then, unless she'd been tied to the chair, it was likely they'd been done from photographs. Normally the portraits hung on the sitting room wall but her father had brought them into the studio. For reference. In both her hair was short, flaxen and neat, held back with a clasp. Disappointingly, her hair had since darkened to what goes by fair or dishwater blonde. The flaxen locks were gone forever.

Also brought in for reference was a group painting, done some years back. A winter scene; night. Lamps cast long, sulphur yellow beams across a frozen pond. Skaters, and their long, flighty shadows arced across the ice. Figures representing Gala and her father were included in the scene. Whereas all the other skaters were poised and graceful, Gala was depicted as a knock-kneed, ungainly, fearful novice, being helped onto the ice by her father.

She doesn't remember her father offering assistance. She remembers his sheepskin jacket and Dr Zhivago hat. She remembers how difficult it was to walk over lumpy frozen ground, ankles jarring at every step, the sharp bands of pressure on the soles of her feet and the icy brightness of the night. But she's not at all sure that her father offered a helping hand. How things are on canvas is not necessarily how they were.

Is it going to be much longer? I can't sit much longer.

Nearly done.

How much longer?

I said I'm nearly done. You can't rush art.

The studio was hot and stuffy, the sun was beating down through the skylight, the air was blue with cigarette smoke and she was stuck sitting for a portrait she'd probably hate.

Okay, he said, that'll do for today.

He stepped back from the easel and squinted at the canvas.

A life study, that's what people want. And sitting for the artist is part of the attraction!

Paint it Black

ON THE LAST night of the dreary summer holidays when the lyrics of 'Sunny Afternoon' and 'Paint it Black' had tunneled wordworms through Gala's brain, her father called her into the studio.

I don't have to sit again, do I?

No, no. That's all done with. I've something to show you.

On the canvas he pulled out from behind the easel was the portrait of a young woman who had, in terms of looks, everything Gala had ever wanted: a smooth, golden complexion, a soft full mouth, a straight narrow nose, delicately arched eyebrows above huge indigo pools and the whole face framed by curtains of hair, smooth and pale as corn silk.

Who is it?

My daughter. As good as. Give or take.

What daughter are you talking about?

Don't be silly. I only have one daughter. That I know of.

That's not me!

It's an artistic *impression*. A portrait doesn't have to be an exact likeness, he said. It's close enough. You have blonde, well *fair* hair. Blue eyes. Not perhaps quite so large, or deep in colour, or symmetrical. I just made one or two adjustments for the sake of the overall effect.

It's not me!

Close enough. It will make an attractive demonstration piece. I can pass it off as you. If potential clients like what they see, they'll cough up. That's what matters.

But who is it really and why do you want to pretend she's me?

It's not *pretending*. It's an *idealised interpretation*.

What's wrong with me as I am?

You're missing the point. This. Just. Turned out. To be. A better composition.

WHO IS IT?

Keep your hair on. It's nobody. It doesn't matter who it is.

WHO IS IT?

He handed over a sticky, smudged picture, torn out of a colour supplement.

There. I based my painting on her. Some model or other.

But that, that's The Shrimp!

Who?

Don't you even know who The Shrimp is?

Haven't a clue. What kind of ridiculous name is that?

The Shrimp is... The Shrimp! Her hair's usually light brown. She's dyed it.

I used my imagination too, by the way. It doesn't matter who she is in real life. It's an *artistic rendering*. It's not just a *copy* of a photograph.

No?

I don't like your tone. *Interpretation* is involved. Interpretation is the point. Anybody can copy a photograph. What does it matter who it is? It's no skin off your nose.

It's not my nose you've painted. Not my eyes, not my mouth, not my hair, not my complexion. And it's definitely not my cleavage!

No need for that kind of language.

I don't have a *cleavage!*

Hold your tongue if you know what's good for you. I'm pleased with the painting and that's all that matters.

But this, this *nobody* is one of the top models in the whole country. Maybe even the world. And she looks NOTHING LIKE ME!

She's got better colouring, certainly. And very neat, regular features. As a matter of fact, I wasn't happy with the painting I did of you. I scrapped it.

Dust rose from the floor as Gala shifted around the limited floor space of studio, trying to find a piece of blank wall to glower at. There wasn't any. Every inch of wall space was taken up with sketches of clothed people she knew and unclothed people most of whom she didn't, though there was one drawing, a standing female nude, with short, bobbed hair and perky little breasts. It could have been Rosetta. It was almost certainly Rosetta.

In a corner of the skylight a fly buzzed and struggled to extricate itself from a spider web. The fly kept on trying the same moves over and over. The same instinct for escape kicking in. The same waste of effort.

I sat for you six times. Six times! You said I had to sit because you needed a painting of me! Your daughter! From life!

Well now I don't. See it as a useful lesson on how it goes in the artistic business. There's a lot of wastage. I intend to pass off this portrait as my daughter so I'd appreciate it if you'd button your lip if you happen to run into any of my acquaintances. Just a bit of artistic licence. No harm done, eh?

Likely Lass

ON A POSTCARD advertising SALTY DOG COCKTAILS! and featuring a garish screenprint of a grinning, winking, jolly old tar:

Dear Mum and Dad,
Guess what? I've just been on a fishing trip! I was
working on a trawler as a deckhand and cook. The boat
was called Likely Lass so I thought it would be okay!
We were a hundred miles out to sea at one point and
there was a storm. The skipper had to see to something
that was in danger of breaking and I had to take over
at the steering wheel and managed to turn the boat
from facing northwest to southeast – which didn't
make me very popular! – but the skipper got us back
on course. The work was very hard, round the clock,
and some of the meals I cooked didn't go down too
well with the crew. They were okay about it, though,
very gentlemanly in fact. They were from the south and
called me ma'am all the time. Anyway I made good
money from the trip so I'm heading off to Mexico
before I'm tempted to spend my earnings here.

The storm at sea was truly terrifying, the boat tossing around like a bath toy, all however many tons an eighty-five-foot trawler weighed in at. The helplessness, isolation, the slim chance of survival if Gala fell overboard, being so small in the scale of things, the vastness of the sea, the very real possibility of drowning and nobody ever finding her. Who'd have gone looking? Only a couple of new friends even knew the name of the boat, and who could say for certain she'd actually gone to sea?

Women on boats were considered unlucky. It was mainly because the skipper had ulterior motives that he took her on and even after a week of not washing and the stink of fish saturating every pore in her body, he was still interested. She couldn't say she hadn't used feminine charms for the sake of some work and even if she'd worked her arse off – which she'd certainly done and had new muscles on her upper arms and thighs to prove it – she was pushing her luck. And a woman on board was pushing the skipper's luck.

At the height of the storm she was so afraid she prayed; Gala the unbeliever, the atheist from childhood, prayed to a God whose existence she denied, a jealous God, an angry God, a God who allowed evil and pain as part of His Plan. She even sang what she remembered of a Redemption Song from the days of accompanying her mother to the church in Yoker:

> *Let the lower lights be burning,*
> *send a gleam across the wave,*
> *Some poor faint and struggling seaman,*
> *you may shelter, you may save.*

They were way too far out for lower lights. Other than the boat's own lights, there was nothing but darkness and deep distance. No shore in sight. She had become a faint and struggling seaman to be sheltered and saved. And not just from the waves.

Gino's

GALA WAS THE first to hear about it. She and whoever else was in Gino's that day.

A one man show! McLellan Galleries! A one man show!

That's good, she said, not because she was clear what her father meant but because he was grinning like he'd won The Pools. And because a lack of response might have been construed as insolence and perceived insolence could turn his smile into a snarl as quick as a struck match could flare.

The caff was a fug of fag smoke and steam. It was noisy: the usual crockery and utensil clatters, the hiss and spit of the coffee machine, the scrape of chairs on lino, the ding-dong of the doorbell but most of all it was noisy from chat. Folk talked in Gino's, the staff even more than the customers. The waiters illustrated their speech with arm waving, shoulder shrugging and eyebrow jiggling. You had to see them talk to hear them properly; to match the actions to the language, a thick tweed of Bargan and Glaswegian, slangy and cadenced, rising and falling like the Tuscan hills she knew from Pliny, or the Kilpatrick hills she knew from family outings.

Geeza cafe alla crema. Anna portiona chips. An for ze senora, a wee Jammie Dodger anna cuppa char.

The waiters' crisp shirts were snow bright. Gold chains glinted at their throats. Their black hair was thick and glossy –

they were free with the Brylcreem – and chins blue well before five o'clock.

The McLellan Galleries. A one man show!

Her father was bouncing on the balls of his feet and flapping his arms. Ready for lift-off. He wasn't addressing Gala, or anyone else. He was simply airing his good news. Loudly. A couple of waiters paused in what they were doing, in case they had a bampot on their hands. Visitations from bampots were not unusual. The door would burst open and someone – usually a man, though the town had its fair share of wild women – would stake out the entranceway and proclaim that the end of the world was nigh, the permissive society was the spawn of the devil, the Reds had crawled out from under the bed or smashed through the Iron Curtain with the express intention of brainwashing the chattering coffee drinkers and turning their kids into informers, that a fleet of UFOs had landed on Glasgow Green and that the dishevelled creature addressing them had first-hand experience of some or all of these imminent calamities.

A one man show! Not before time, if I say so myself. I've served my dues, oh yes but this just might be the clincher!

He was lit up, buzzing like a power station. But hadn't yet graduated to the league of total bampots. The waiters shook their heads, did some reciprocal shrugging and resumed their balletic floorshow.

Have to go and see a man about some frames. No time like the present. Here, he said, pulling a note from his pocket. Treat yourself. And find something useful to do until I get back. Homework? Revision?

Still grinning, he bounded towards the door.

A ten bob note, when half a crown would have been more than enough!

Gala ordered coffee and chocolate cake. The waiter was not tall, but undeniably dark and handsome. He smiled and called her *Signorina*, which was a big improvement on *Miss* and gave her belly flutters. Easy to spend an hour in Gino's while her father went off to confer with a picture framer. At least he wouldn't need a set of scary villain shots to advertise an exhibition. If photos were required at all, they'd want something friendly, thoughtful or appealingly eccentric.

For a man who'd been calling himself an artist for as long as she could remember, her father wasn't one for introducing the family to the genius of Old Masters, far less any up-and-coming talent. When did he ever encourage her to look beyond homemade, homespun art?

In spite of a growing awareness that he didn't match up to the flamboyant free spirit typically associated with his calling – if not so much with teaching, the day job which paid the bills – she still harboured the notion of some day following in her father's footsteps and trying her hand as an artist.

But did she have the talent? And what exactly was talent, and how could you access it? On his last visit, the school chaplain had once again rehashed the parable of the talents. When he reached the part about seeds falling on barren soil, a ripple of sniggers and giggles passed through his audience of three hundred adolescent girls. He compared wasted talents to miniskirts, smoking and loose morals. His words fell on stony ground. But the seeds, the talents had to have existed in the first place. How hard could it be to use them properly? She had a sketch pad in her bag but first there was homework. There was always homework, and tests, and revisions, and O-levels basking in the middle distance with their fins up and teachers who never failed to find ways to remind their classes on a daily basis of the slow but unstoppable approach of the inevitable.

What did she have that day? A problem relating to the speed of light from *Physics is Fun*? Writing up a class experiment involving the conversion of starch to sugar? Translating Pliny's commentary on one of Caesar's military campaigns? Conjugating irregular French verbs, trying to get to grips with a chunk of *Romeo and Juliet*?

The waiter brought coffee and cake, slipped the bill under the saucer, once again addressed her as *Signorina* and broke into a snatch of Puccini as he returned to the serving hatch, head held high, shiny shoes gliding across the chequered floor. Gala ate some cake, then did some homework. Surrounded by Italian waiters, the Latin translation wasn't as dismal as usual. These handsome, well-pressed men were descendants of the Romans and the language they spoke a descendant of Latin. Perhaps she could ask the waiter for help with Caesar's campaign?

Art that day had not, for once, been cancelled. The art teacher, Miss Liffey, was often *indisposed,* and even when she was present, she gave the impression of being on the point of collapse or of suffering a fit of anachronistic vapours. Unfortunately the same couldn't be said for rest of the staff. The Latin mistress, ancient as the Colosseum, frequently nodded off at her desk, her splayed knees revealing salmon pink bloomers. But she could always spot a collaborative translation, and never missed a class. Nor did the big, brash French teacher, who regaled the class with holiday adventures featuring *pastis,* continental transport cafés and lorry drivers; nor the bustling battleaxe who taught chemistry; the dried stick of a maths teacher; the floaty Welsh woman who taught physics; nor the clump-footed English teacher whose only love was Shakespeare.

In art, they had been doing figure composition. The model – a burly, heavy-jawed girl – had slouched on a chair against a backdrop of faded velvet curtains. She was a bully, especially on the hockey pitch: her trick was to pretend to be going for the ball then whack the shins of whoever was in her way. Gala wasn't particularly pleased with the drawing but who wanted to draw a big, ugly bully in the first place?

Hmmm, if I were you, I wouldn't set your heart on *art.* Her father was at her shoulder with a sheaf of sample frame materials under his arm and whisky fumes on his breath. I'd concentrate on what you're good at, if I were you.

I got the top mark in art.

From that Liffey woman? Wouldn't trust her judgement. Airy fairy. Fey.

But I like drawing.

That's as may be. Pack up your stuff and we'll be off. One more stop to make. A flying visit. To Chitti's.

I'll be late for my piano lesson.

You can give it a miss for once. You have my permission.

But I've got an exam next week!

And I've got a one man show coming up. It's all a question of priorities.

Is your show next week?

Of course not. Don't be ridiculous.

I need the lesson. I'm not ready.

If you're not ready now, you never will be.

When it came to piano exams, it was practise and practise and even when you could play a piece without a single mistake you had to practise more because things could go wrong on the day, on an unfamiliar piano in a high-ceilinged room in the Athenaeum where everything sounded different. The chair might not be at the right height, the keys might be slippery from all the other fingers which had tapped at them, an open window could usher in the sirens of fire engines or ambulances, or starlings – a murmuration of starlings could make a hell of a racket. But nerves were the worst. Nerves could really make you mess up.

And no matter what went wrong – you misheard the adjudicator, thought he asked for a G minor arpeggio when in fact he asked for G flat major, the sight reading was a rash of accidentals, no matter what stupid little thing knocked you off – the only acceptable outcome was *a good mark*.

Mrs Hammond might have been sympathetic about nerves, feeling off colour, sweaty palms or a mean adjudicator. No excuse was acceptable to her mother and father; a bad result was good money wasted. Yet here was her father suggesting she skip class a week before the exam.

It was years since she'd last been to the foundry. The road from the city centre was long and drab: rows of rag stores and bargain warehouses; a trail of closing-down sales; throngs of manky pigeons. Even from inside the car she could smell chip fat and pubs and something dank and rotten off the river.

This'll make them sit up and take note, said her father. Not before time, oh no, high time it happened and this is just the beginning. I may have started later than some – I've got my family to answer for that – but somebody, somebody at the McLellan Galleries, no less, has seen my talent, recognised my artistic merit. Chitti will be impressed.

Chitti wasn't around. He was in Italy, on family business. His replacement had the same chunky torso, heavy shoulders and pendulous arms, the same doleful eyes.

Tell Chitti to contact me the moment he returns, said her father. I'm going to need his assistance straight away!

Very good, sir.

Straight away. I've got a one man show at the McLellan Galleries. All systems go! He has my number. Price. Miles Price.

With a stub of pencil, the man wrote something in a battered notebook.

Sure you've got the name?

Aye. Price.

You might be hearing more of it. Yes, indeed.

He drove home past the street where Gala was born. The whole area, the neat, well-planned grid seemed so small and quaint, almost too picturesque for its own good, a trim and tidy enclave within a shabby sprawl of tenements and beyond them, poking at the grey sky, the concrete high-rises of Yoker.

D'you ever wish you still lived here, Dad?

No fear. Just taking a shortcut to the switchback.

Pelmanism

IN THE FRONT room, Gala set up the card table in front of the gas fire and laid out the pack, face down. It was a stormy night. Stray branches of cupressus rapped against the window. Thunder grumbled in the distance. Once in a while, the lights dipped. Ever since her father's fling with amateur dramatics, a dip in the lights meant only one thing: *Gaslight! A Victorian Melodrama in three acts*. Miles as Mr Manningham, villain of the piece, the bad man in the attic. His wife, poor browbeaten Bella, at the end of her tether. The saucy callous maid, the plodding but supportive detective. When Manningham was rummaging around the attic in search of some jewels, the gaslight dipped. When he left the attic and returned 'home' – though in fact he'd never left the premises, just nipped up a back staircase to the attic – the lights went up again. A simple but effective stage device.

Her father was out in the studio, working up a painting. Jas was sleeping over at a friend's. Her mother had gone off to do some organ practice at the local church. Gala and Gran had the house to themselves. It was rare for them to spend time together in the front room. The back of the house was their territory, Gran to-ing and fro-ing from the kitchen, Gala at the table in the dinette, with homework or drawing, or the two of them together on the couch, watching TV. Gran was for setting up the cards in the dinette but, in the hope of preserving some sense of occasion, Gala persuaded her to stick to the usual arrangement.

Gran had been looking forward to a visit from Lil and Win. It had been months since the last time they'd made it out of town. In preparation, Gala had done her hair: shampoo, curlers, Amami setting lotion, a soft brush to style it when dry. After Gran had cleared up the tea dishes, taken off her apron and put on her best dress – calf-length lilac knit with a lurex thread through it – after she had powdered her nose and smiled in the mirror at the contrived fullness of her hair, Lil had phoned to say that her legs were giving her gyp and she didn't feel she could risk the four flights of tenement stairs twice in one night. Win had also called off. She'd cracked her dentures on a lamb chop and couldn't thole the mortification of being seen on the bus with a caved-in face.

We're aw fallin apairt, said Gran. Our auld banes are gien up the ghost. Even oor dentures are throwin in the towel, she joked, but there was no mistaking her disappointment.

Gran was old. A modest celebration for her eightieth birthday was in the offing; nothing fancy, just a nice lunch in town. Her own brothers and sisters were already dead and only a handful of contemporaries were still on the go. Even if there had been plenty friends and family to help her celebrate, Gran would have protested at any extravagance on her account. A roof over her head and the opportunity to make herself useful was, she insisted, as much as any penniless widow could hope for.

Gala had already bought presents: a lilac silk scarf from Marks & Sparks, soft and floaty as a summer breeze and, to satisfy her sweet tooth, a box of Newberry Fruits.

I hope Lil's legs pick up, said Gran. Sooner or later she'll havetae gae ower the door. The last time she wis poorly, she sent her poor brither for bread and marge and whit did he come back wi? Bleach and shoe polish. They didny hae a bite tae eat for three days! Hopeless. Knows it tae. A terrible thing tae know ye're hopeless.

Over the years, Gala had been to the homes of Win and Lil several times. The journeys involved a tram or trolleybus ride, a hike up endless flights of stairs but there was always a beaming welcome at the top, a gust of warm, fusty air, a scone or a slab of fruit cake, a pat on the head, a glass of something – milk, coffee, a wee sherry – Lil and Win had been offering Gala a wee sherry since she was eight – and always compliments: What lovely hair! How tall! How grown up! How clever!

Gala was let loose to poke around a recently dusted and thoroughly polished sitting room, crammed with knick-knacks and keepsakes and cumbersome furniture. In Win's, an anaemic canary hopped from one perch to another; in Lil's, a stooped, silent brother sat in a dim corner, darning socks. There was always a comfy window seat where she could do her homework, draw, daydream or gaze down at the trundle of street life far below.

Old as they were, the ladies laughed. How they laughed! Light, frothy effusions, bubbling up from a gentle stream of conversation. And if they spoke of sad things, they leaned towards each other's lambswool twinsets and ample skirts, dropped their voices to a murmur and held the sad words between them so that Gala, the ever-growing, ever-precious child, might be spared.

This is nice, said Gran, pouring them both a small sherry and shuffling the cards. Whit'll it be, then?

Pelmanism?

Right ye are.

Gran always let Gala have her way.

Canny mind the last time I played Pelmanism, she added, and laughed at the joke of what she'd said.

Pelmanism is a memory game. The aim is to collect pairs of cards until the board is cleared. The entire pack is laid out, face down. In turn, each player picks two cards. If they make a pair, the cards are removed and added to the player's pile. If not, they are replaced, face down, in their original position. The skill is in memorising where certain cards lie, and improving on chance. The winner is the player who accumulates the greatest number of pairs.

Gran was usually good at the game but that night she was making mistakes, silly mistakes, and Gala was winning too easily. Maybe she was thinking about her friends who couldn't make it. When Gala was little, and she'd had a bad run of luck, Gran would find a way to let her back into the game, give her a fighting chance. Gala considered making a couple of deliberate mistakes, letting Gran win a game or two, in the hope it might cheer her up but somehow her ploy didn't feel right.

Through the wall, her father shifted around. Marlene was belting out a number about the black market being just around the corner.

Miles better mind he doesny overdo it, said Gran.

Her father had been putting in all the hours he could find to prepare for his one man show. If he hadn't had to drive into the city five days a week to carry out his teaching duties, he'd have shacked up in the studio. To say he was happy wouldn't be accurate. Gala can't think of a time when her father could have been described as happy; but he was engaged, absorbed, and that, for everybody, was a good thing.

Lightning jagged through a gap in the curtains. Branches clawed at the window. Thunder cracked overhead.

Mercy, said Gran, looking up at the ceiling. Sounds like the roof's gonny cave in. Like the blitz. Cheers, dearie.

They clinked glasses and each took a sip of sherry. The thunder cracked again. Gran jolted in her seat, righted herself then said brightly:

Yon table frae Granny Price needs a polish. Remind me it needs doin, will ye?

Can't Mum do it? You do too much. And on your birthday you've to do nothing at all but eat, drink and be merry. And wear a nice dress.

Yir mither's got her hands full. Besides, yon table's a thorn in the flesh for Vera, and for Miles tae, even mair for Miles. Ye canny aye write aff aw the wrangs that have been done tae ye. And yir faither hurts mair than he lets on. Naebody's perfect. And hurt can turn tae bitterness – Where's ma queen? Where's she hiding? Ach, wrang again. Dear, Dear. The grey matter's rottin away like an auld mop. Aye, that's whit I've got for a heid now, an auld rotten mop, no even good for washin the flerr. No screwed on right. Ma queen, where's ma queen, where's she aff tae? Ma queenie's gone, God love us, upped and left, aff wi the raggle taggle gyps, flitted wi her flerr mop, forsaken her feather bed, her mop heid, her grey matter, her lingo's lost by jings her lingo's run amok, it's a daft dog, a dog gone berserk, a lingo bingo stupit auld bane brain –

Gala had never heard Gran talk rubbish like this, never heard her talk any kind of rubbish at all, or seen her stiffen and rear out of the chair, her blue eyes black and frozen.

Deadlines

WITHOUT GRAN STEERING the family through its own deep waters, the house tipped and rolled. The stroke had left her paralysed down one side: she could barely speak or eat, far less do anything else for herself and after a few days, her room began to smell of illness. Vera opened the windows, scooshed perfume around: Sea Jade, *a new, fresh fragrance with a hint of the Far East,* and packaged in a gold and turquoise canister. Behind the mask of Sea Jade, the smell of illness continued to lurk.

The effects of the stroke didn't go away. Not only had it caused physical debility, it had short-circuited part of Gran's brain so her words came out slurred and confused. She tried writing down what she wanted to say but what she wrote, though shot through with glimpses of clarity, didn't always make sense: *Good girls are toadstools. The queen says bow-bow. There's a bucketful o fairies if ye're famished.*

The doctor visited regularly, with his hushed tones, black bag, swabs and morphine. The family became even more fragmented than before. Each of them took a turn sitting with the invalid. The TV was moved into Gran's room and set up next to a faded photo of her long-gone husband – so young, so gangly, such a far-reaching gaze – and the even more faded photo of herself as a serious, curly-headed child in a long smock and ankle boots. Nobody was sure what Gran could still see or hear but the TV was always on for her favourite programmes: *Hancock's Half Hour, Coronation Street, Steptoe and Son*. If nothing else, it provided something for her visitors to look at other than poor old Gran with her droopy eye and cracked lips. And something to talk about: *Is the TV too loud, too quiet? Is the picture clear enough? Is that a repeat? Look what Harold's up to now! You never liked that Elsie Tanner, did you? Shall I change the channel?*

Gran's responses were vague, hard to make out. For the first time, as far as Gala remembers, her mother took charge of the household chores. Gala and Jas helped out. Up to high doh about exhibition deadlines and slacking pupils, and suffering withdrawals from golf, swimming and other therapeutic activities, Miles increased his cigarette, coffee and whisky intake and continued to burn the midnight oil. Time was tight. Work had to be varnished, mounted, framed and ready to go. Soon. Very soon. A deadline was a deadline.

For the time being, Vera cancelled her piano teaching. Lah Lahing along to 'Für Elise' or 'La Fille aux Cheveux du Lin' while her mother was dying was out of the question. And Gran *was* dying. Everybody knew but nobody mentioned it, nobody said the word out loud. Especially anywhere near Gran, as if it were best she didn't know how ill she was, as if being deceived into imagining she might pull through until there was no time to make her peace, to settle old scores or whatever else she might have felt her last moments should be used for, was how it should be.

The unknown wishes of a dying person were put aside in favour of the living, the still living, the outliving, who knew best: after all, it was they who had to soldier on; to deal with the inevitable unspoken eventuality. And its aftermath. Even if there were times when sense seemed irretrievably lost in Gran's brain, there were times when she knew exactly what was happening; she knew, for example, when Gala and her mother eased her onto the commode, that she was helpless in the face of humiliation.

Vera tried to persuade Miles to postpone his show. Until. But no-one could be sure how long it might be before *until* became *when*. If Gran's heart was strong, it was possible, the doctor said, that she might stay alive for some considerable time. Not so likely, perhaps, but possible all the same. And possible that the Prices would find themselves caring for a confused, helpless old woman who had once been the warm, hard-working heart of the family.

There was, however, the doctor's brown bag, his hypodermic needles, his free hand with analgesics. There was morphine: douser of misery, stifler of pain, the poppy pillow. There was talk of putting the patient out of her misery. Gala was not invited into any discussions on the matter but made it her business to eavesdrop on any *sotto voce* parley the doctor held with her parents.

The minister also visited the house with his sombre smile, the slow, considered removal of his hat, the pensive weighing of it on flat palms. He was shown into the sickroom where two chairs and a side table had been set up for visitors. He was offered tea, coffee, something stronger. Usually the Reverend Balquidder took tea: *Milk and three sugars, please. Sweetness is my weakness* – but one dismal afternoon he agreed to something stronger – *Neat, thank you. No need to gild the lily.* Having little experience of pouring strong drink, as Miles always attended to his own refreshments, Vera half-filled the minister's tumbler.

On previous visits the minister had brought along his old dog, an arthritic black lab which had accompanied him on countless errands of mercy, dragging its stiff tail across the hallways of the parish, but that day the man came alone. He brought comfort in distress, the mothwing whirr of his gold-leafed bible, the practised patience of one whose calling is to listen to God and console troubled souls.

After he had spent half an hour with Gran, it was usual for Vera to poke her head into the sickroom, ostensibly to offer more refreshment but in fact to give the minister an opportunity to take his leave; that day she sent Gala in. Jas had a test the following day and she was quizzing him on his ability to identify subordinate clauses within complex sentences. Jas found schoolwork more difficult than Gala but Vera believed that if he applied himself more assiduously, he too would attain top marks, which were the only marks she considered acceptable. The household might have been in the throes of impending bereavement but that was no excuse for letting educational standards slip.

The minister was holding an empty glass and staring into space. *The Sooty Show* was on the TV. The volume was turned down. Sweep was bashing Sooty over the head with his magic wand. Sooty was whacking Sweep with stiff, furry arms. Gran was fast asleep. And considering her frail condition, snoring rather loudly. And dribbling from the frozen side of her mouth. Why hadn't the man taken his leave? How dare he sit watching a helpless old woman trying to get some rest?

Gala ushered him through the hall, handed him his hat and slammed the door at his back. It was not until later in the day that she learned the reason for his reluctance to shift himself: before visiting the afflicted, the Reverend Balquidder had taken his dog to the vet's. Due to the discovery of an inoperable tumour, the minister had consented for his loyal companion to be put down. While Gran slept, he had been mourning his dog, blowtorching his grief with neat whisky. Gala felt the prickle of guilt, and something like sympathy.

Gran's friends also came to visit, armed with bunches of daffs and tulips, seedless grapes, pokes of soft sweeties and quivery smiles. Lil hobbled in on swollen legs. Win clicked her new plate back into position, adjusted her wig and straightened her specs before entering the sickroom, to look her best for a lifelong friend who was at her worst. The old ladies came separately. And together. Whenever they could. There was none of the bustle and fluster of Patience nights, no tinkly giggles, no reckless smudges of lipstick and glittery brooches. They kept their coats on, even though it was spring and the weather was mild, kept their cardigans buttoned up and seemed to shrink into themselves, to become hushed and meek as church mice.

On their way out, they pressed Gala to their woolly bosoms before departing solemnly, heads bowed.

Friends of Vera's also came to visit, long-standing friends whose own parents were ailing, fading, falling apart, losing the place, in their second childhood. Beattie McCord made several visits, cheerful and resilient as ever. Due to the demands of her own large family, Beattie could never stay long but always brought with her a crackle of energy and an unshakeable conviction in the goodness of God. On one occasion, her daughter Ailsa accompanied her. Ailsa and Gala, who had given each other a wide berth since the dawning of Gala's atheism, wandered down the garden together, trying but failing to find anything to talk about.

Miles mostly managed to confine his relentless pacing to his studio. His own visits to the sickroom were brief. Did he tell his mother-in-law about how the work for his exhibition was progressing, list the influential contacts he had invited to the opening? Did he reminisce about his own mother, at whose end he was absent, or busy himself with opening or closing a window, adjusting a curtain, plumping a pillow until he was satisfied that he had done all he could and, therefore, might as well get back to work?

Jas brought Gran bunches of wildflowers from his forays in the woods, where he went whenever he was able to escape his mother's close attention to his homework. Tongue-tied, he stood at her bedside, eyes darting between her frozen face and the TV, clutching his posies so tightly that he crushed the delicate stems. When Gala found a vase for his flowers, he bolted.

Gran deteriorated. She confused Gala with Vera, Miles with Grandad Price. She drifted between decades, dropped off mid-sentence, came to with a start and a surge of panic. She developed bedsores. Her lips cracked. Being bathed caused her pain. Being fed caused her pain. Being moved caused her pain. Not being moved caused her pain.

Miles continued teaching and agonising about his forthcoming exhibition. Invitations had already been sent out and so postponement was to be avoided at all costs. It was too much of a risk to even consider asking the gallery directors if they might change the date. Who could tell how they'd respond? They might be sympathetic to his situation; then again, they had a business to run, art to sell, money to make. He'd waited long enough to hang his work on the reputable walls of the McLellan Galleries. The opportunity might never come again.

Sea Jade

GRAN'S DEATH HAPPENED quietly, at home. Was it another stroke, an overly generous dose of morphine? Was there any pronouncement on the cause of death? Gala had heard murmurs about problems with breathing, vital organs beginning to shut down, about her helpless and hopeless condition. Whatever the cause, for a woman who abhorred the very thought of being a burden on anyone, in any way, at any time, her end was merciful. She died on her eightieth birthday.

There followed the throwing wide of the bedroom windows. Spring air skirled in, lifting the fringes of the faded antimacassars crocheted by the itinerant Anastasia. Vases of wilted flowers were removed. The commode was removed. Then the body. After the undertaker's van had left the driveway, Vera dragged Gran's bedding into the back garden and set it alight. It burned for hours, sent a coil of filthy smoke around the neighbourhood. She followed the bonfire with a flurry of scrubbing and polishing. The TV was reinstated in the living room. Nobody felt like watching *Coronation Street*, *Steptoe and Son* or *Hancock's Half Hour* for long enough.

Gala has no memory of a funeral but it must have been a cremation. Long before she became ill, Gran had stated her wish to be turned to ash: *Nae point in ma auld banes takkin up guid grund.* There must have been a service. Hymns and prayers and sodden hankies. A small, subdued congregation. Old lady voices wobbling around the high notes of the hymns. A eulogy from Reverend Balquidder, praising Gran's devotion to her only daughter's family, the selfless labour she had offered for little reward beyond a roof over her head and seeing her grandchildren grow. Coughs and shoe-shuffling during the prayers. The dull thud of the minister's voice hitting bare wood pews, the flagstone floor. Mumbled, staggered *Amens*. Hugs and handshakes at the door. Tea and sandwiches in the function room of a hotel near the crematorium, which specialised in such gloomy gatherings.

Nothing. No sense of having been there, taken part. Did she really stay away – how could she have, why would she have, what could possibly have been so pressing? Did her mother discourage her for attending, fearing that a visit to the crematorium might have a detrimental effect on exam performance? Was she beside herself with grief? What on earth did she do with the day? And where was Jas? If she didn't go, surely Jas wouldn't have been the only child at the funeral? Why is it all such a blank?

Gala does remember that while her mother was clearing and airing Gran's room, she developed an acute aversion to Sea Jade. She managed to persuade her mother to throw out a perfectly good, half-full canister of the stuff and molecule by molecule, the scent departed from the house. With the exception of her bible, her engagement, wedding and eternity rings, a keepsake or two – of purely sentimental value – so too did Gran's few possessions.

When Gala returned to school, however, the scent hit her like a slap in the face. Miss Nantucket, the clunking, heavy-footed English teacher, had taken to dousing herself in the stuff. Even from across the classroom, or from the far end of a corridor, amid the clotted odours of adolescent girls and menopausal spinsters, Sea Jade turned Gala's stomach and constricted her breathing.

After months, years of tests and revision and sample papers, of nagging and threats and dire warnings, the O-levels were just around the corner. Miss Nantucket called Gala out to her desk to collect a corrected revision exercise. She'd done badly. The work was sloppy. Not at all what was expected of her. This was no time to let extraneous circumstances get in the way of performance. Gala wasn't listening or caring. She was thinking about the loss of her Gran, the great gaping hole in the family that opened when she died. And trying not to breathe. As the teacher handed back her script, inducing an additional blast of Sea Jade, Gala blurted out the perfume problem.

Well, really! said Miss Nantucket. Here I am trying to add a note of freshness to this stuffy old place and one of my pupils has to kick up a fuss about my choice of scent! You, young lady, will just have to learn to live with it. And regarding your revision exercise, I suggest you keep your outlandish opinions on Lady Macbeth to yourself and make more use of *Coles Notes*.

Gooseberries

ON A UK aerogramme plastered with small denomination stamps:

Dear Gala,
    We have more or less settled into the new house and
have begun to sort out the garden, which has been let to
run wild. Your father bought a new hedge trimmer and
has been slashing his way through the foliage. He seems
to enjoy the work. I have planted some rose bushes
and some hardy perennials. It has been a disappointing
summer, a great deal of rain and overcast days, but
the gooseberries are thriving. I'm not overly fond of
gooseberries but there's enough for goodness knows
how much jam, so I'll have to look out Gran's old
jeelypan.
    It wasn't as much of a wrench leaving the west as I
thought it was going to be and under the circumstances,
it was the only alternative. I hope to be able to keep in
touch with Beattie McCord and some of my other old
friends. Your father seems content enough to burn his
boats. I hope this new start will buck him up.
    We are running in the new car – a bottle green Audi.
I'd prefer him not to drive at all but he's insistent. He

can't abide being in the car with me behind the wheel. And to be honest, his carping doesn't help my driving.

Your father has been put on some new medication which seems to be working but does make him rather withdrawn. He has taken up modelmaking and has ordered kits for a Hawker Hurricane and a Supermarine Spitfire. He's already assembled an Avro Lancaster and an Armstrong Whitworth Whitley. He hasn't touched a canvas for months. What he has here is more of a workshop than a studio though it has plenty of light for painting and where there's a will there's a way.

Your brother has been up and down lately, more down than up, not that I can see what he's got to be down about. On the plus side, I suspect that he has met someone else but he tells me very little about his personal life. I do hope she turns out to be better than you know who. The custody battle is ongoing and I'm sure it can't do anybody any good.

I have started a primary teaching job in a nearby village school. The children are on the slow side, but biddable. The schools here still have an autumn break so the children can help bring in the tatties. It's heartening to see children helping their parents.

Hope you are well and that we will see you soon.

Love from Mum (and Dad, of course).

P.S. Did the money order reach you safely? Do let me know. I hate to think of money going astray.

One Man Show

THERE WAS A crowd. A small crowd. *A select gathering*, though a number of people are missing from her memory. Jas, for one. Where was he? He wore a gingham shirt and long trousers, navy corduroy. How can she remember what he wore when she can't place him at her father's one man show? Beattie and Lou must have been there. Unlike some, who came up with inventive excuses as to why they couldn't attend, Beattie wouldn't have failed to show up unless one of her brood was in mortal danger. The neighbours too, the Billingses and the Douglases, they were there. She knows they were. The Douglases were the first to buy a painting: a sunset over water. The Billingses bought a wood carving of a cat. Gala has seen the sunset and the cat in their new homes. She walks round the memory again: such an echoey, high-ceilinged room. The guests swim in and out of focus.

On the drinks table stood bottles of whisky, gin, sherry, a soda syphon, a jug of squash and a large bowl of peanuts. The space was airy. Natural light streamed through the tall windows. Miles, the man of the moment, suitably spruced up – safari jacket, tangerine shirt with paisley cravat – and a fizzing cocktail of exhilaration and nervous tension, dotted from one cluster of people to another. The low hum of conversation was intermittently embellished by the chink of glasses and the raising of a toast: *Cheers! Bottoms up! Down the hatch! Chin chin!* High heels clicked against polished parquet, flowery perfumes mingled with spicy aftershave. Fortunately for Gala, nobody was wearing Sea Jade.

Three men. Around her father's age. Florid faces, whisky breath, nostril hair. They didn't introduce themselves, just strolled up, swilling drinks and launched right in:

So you're the daughter, eh?

Heard a lot about you.

Oh yes, Miles isn't one for sparing the details.

Nudge, nudge, tap, tap at a veined nose, stroke, stroke at a stubbled chin, pick, pick, pick between tobacco-stained teeth.

A lot about you, yes indeed. All that talent at your fingertips.

Chip off the old block, eh?

Can't say better than that, can you?

Some might have qualms about offspring following in their footsteps.

Sprogs leapfrogging over their elders and betters.

Outshining them.

Putting them in the shade.

Always a possibility. Always a possibility.

Did he say I had talent? Did my dad really say that?

Oh yes. Absolutely. Heaps of it. But your father's a talented man himself. No need to fear a comeuppance from the fruit of his loins, no, no.

Indeed. Those views of Loch Lomond are grand.

Absolutely first class.

You really feel you're there, don't you? Sitting on a rock, sunning yourself and admiring the view.

Dad doesn't do sunny scenes, Gala pointed out. He prefers overcast days. Dirty-coloured days.

Well, yes, dear, you've got a point. But then there's his skill as a sculptor, too. Me, I wouldn't know one end of a chisel from the other.

They say a sculptor actually sees the form in the block of wood or stone. That it's there all the time just waiting to be discovered and released.

Sounds like hooey to me.

Claptrap.

Mumbo jumbo.

And too damned easy. When it can't be easy, can it? Not when it takes years of training to learn the techniques.

Before you even begin to think about *artistic inspiration*.

But when it comes to portraiture, I mean, looking at that canvas over there then seeing his lovely daughter right here beside us. In the flesh…

There's a passing resemblance.

Passing, yes, but not what you'd call a photographic likeness. Of course, it's not a photo, so you wouldn't expect that…

A resemblance, and yet –

They looked from Gala to the portrait of The Shrimp then back to Gala.

That's because, Gala mumbled, *because* –

What's that, m'dear? Did you want to say something?

No, she said. No!

The men checked the level of their drinks and found it insufficient.

Miles did say that portrait was of his daughter but he must have been pulling our leg. You know what a joker Miles is.

I remember him flashing that painting around the club. I was hoping for an invitation to meet the sitter!

It's quite clear that the young lady in the painting is rather more… tanned.

And more blonde.

Of course you have to consider artistic licence.

Absolutely. Nobody minds a bit of artistic licence.

And less curvaceous. Skinny in fact. Too skinny, to my mind.

Chaps like more meat on the bone, so to speak.

Don't like our girls to look like they've come out of concentration camps!

Although to tell the truth, the lass in the painting is curvy *where it counts*, if you get my drift.

My Granny Price was a Japanese prisoner of war, said Gala, folding her arms firmly across her nonexistent cleavage. So was Grandad. My granny did hard labour and Grandad was starved and beaten and –

Yes, yes, m'dear, now that I think about it, Miles did mention something of his poor parents' trials. Not that they were the only ones to suffer, not by a long shot. Well, yes –

Yes, if you'll excuse us, m'dear, it's time for us to... circulate. Enjoy yourself, m'dear.

If you can't be good, be careful!

The trio listed towards the drinks table.

What d'you know! the sweatiest one chuckled, lowering his voice so of course Gala listened hard enough to catch every word. Isn't Miles a card? Trying to make out he'd given birth to a goddess!

Small groups were clumped around the room. Now and again somebody would glance at the walls, gesture towards a painting or sculpture but nobody was paying close attention to the art: they were too busy drinking and talking and slapping each other on the back. Apart from Vera, propped between a pair of landscapes featuring hills, reeds and water; playing wallflower. Her mustard dress was neither flattering nor fashionable but the colour did chime with the paintings.

Vera did not enjoy playing wife of the artist. The role appealed to her even less than wife of the leading man, when Miles had been in his amateur dramatics phase. It wasn't that she didn't support his artistic endeavours. Of course she did. As much as any wife could be expected to. Hadn't she put up with dusty footprints on the carpet, the chink of chisels and the squeal of saws, the stink of turps and resins, the filthy jars of paint-logged water? Hadn't she listened to his gripes about the lack of commissions, the cheapskates who asked for something particular then complained about the price? And now she had to put up with God knows who he'd invited from the golf club or the baths or the bars he frequented. People she didn't know and had no inclination to become acquainted with.

Laughter rattled through the high-ceilinged gallery. The source was a woman with wide-set eyes, dramatically defined by lashings of kohl and mascara, and a heart-shaped face set off by a sleek dark bob. Her damson dress was too short for her age, though she was trim enough to just about get away it. Still laughing, in a tone that Vera would have described as common, the woman pulled away from a group gathered round a little bronze head – Jas when he was a sweet, button-nosed babe – and tacked towards the booze. It was Rosetta and she was drunk. Rosetta and Gala's father went back a long way. Her mother had nothing good to say about Rosetta.

Her father broke away from a cluster of folk to whom he'd been holding forth and made a beeline for the drinks table.

Miles, darling! Aren't you clever doing all this, this, this… art! Rosetta flapped around like a leggy bird, then flung her arms around Gala's father. The trio of tipplers continued to chortle and blah but otherwise conversations took a dip. Flushed, grinning tipsily, her father extricated himself from Rosetta's clinch. Stiffer than ever now, more red hot poker than wallflower, Gala's mother glared into the middle distance.

Oh come on, Miles, said Rosetta, loud and clear and undeniably more posh than common. Loosen up. You're an artist, aren't you? Well, some of the time, at least. A free spirit! Or have you sold your soul to the devil of convention? Has being in with the bricks at that dreary old school done for the old devil I used to know and adore? Miles, Miles – what bloody harm can a little smoochy-woochy do, Miles? Old times and all that. No, no – forget that, forget that crap! I couldn't give a monkey's for old times. No time like the present, that's what I say! Give us a kiss, Miles! I'm not suggesting any *hanky panky*! I'm not making an indecent proposal. That would be quite, quite out of the question, wouldn't it? You're a married man. And me, poor old me, I'm a loose, louche woman. A *divorceeeeee!*

Rosetta knocked back her gin and aimed her plump, plummy lips at Gala's father.

Aftermath

PEOPLE CAME. BUT not enough of them. And those who came weren't the right people, the ones who counted. Or, if the right people came, they made the wrong noises. Or no noise at all. Or all the right noises at the time but didn't follow up. Little was sold. Barely enough to cover the cost of framing. After the run of the exhibition, demoted by the absence of a red sticker to the contemptible category of *unsold,* once more works piled up around the house.

Vera did her best. She repeated such positive feedback as there had been over and over, but all it did was irk him. He avoided his studio, spent more and more time at the golf club and had nothing good to say about art or artists or galleries or one man shows. He began floating get-rich-quick schemes again and chewing over strategies about how to break into new social circles. People with principles were what he was after, clear principles, people who believed in rank, order, discipline. Army people. After all, he was an ex-serviceman. He'd been through the war. The fact that his unit had been fortunate enough to miss any real action was neither here nor there. The point was that he'd signed up, done the training, and was ready and willing, if need be, to obey orders – and dish them out as well. That was how the whole thing worked. That was the system.

Called upon to confront the enemy, he would have done his

duty, no doubt about it. He was no coward, turncoat, deserter. That sort, no, he had no truck with that sort. He was loyal, a patriot. Hadn't he stuck by his family – his parents, siblings, his wife and children, his mother-in-law – hadn't he done the right thing by every last one of them? He could have turned his back on his responsibilities and pursued the life of a free spirit, like some he knew, but he wasn't the type for that, though the thought had crossed his mind often enough, oh yes, the joys of a life unencumbered by family had crossed his mind.

The reason why he wasn't reaping the benefits he deserved from all his effort – and nobody put in more effort than he did – was simple: he had been associating with the wrong sort of people, he saw that now, why had he not seen it before when it was staring him in the face? The types who'd started to crawl out of the woodwork, with their wishy-washy ideas about the ways of the world, banging on about egalitarianism, live and let live, all that rot – shirkers and wastrels and workshies, he'd had his fill of them.

It was time to resume contact with men of action, to be back in the midst of his own kind. The fact that he had joined the Indian Army and his outfit was composed mostly of Sikhs was not what he was talking about. Not at all. It was the structure he was talking about. A simple, straightforward hierarchy. Somebody told somebody else what to do and it was done; no questions asked. A man knew his place in the order of things and stuck to it. Each had his part to play. In life, some were leaders, others followers. And if you were a leader – as he certainly considered himself to be – your job was to instil obedience in your subordinates. And that could only be achieved through discipline.

He bought himself a blazer and tartan trews and took out a subscription to *Sporting Life*. He put an advertisement in the local paper: *Ex-serviceman seeks bridge partner.* He displayed a photo of himself and his army outfit on the mantelpiece, along with a couple of medals, which, on Jas's closer inspection, turned out to be from Burma. According to Vera, though she didn't say it while Miles was in earshot, he had never been in Burma.

He bought Jas a pair of boxing gloves and set up a punchbag in the garage. The boy needed toughening up. He didn't want a namby-pamby, sensitive sort for a son. He wanted a boy who had a strong chin, a firm handshake, nerves of steel and a stiff upper lip, who looked a person straight in the eye without blinking like a rabbit. He wanted a boy who was a credit to him, who was tough and loyal, who could take the rough with the smooth and knew what side his bread was buttered on. Jas, who was more interested in roaming the woods on the lookout for injured animals, dutifully laced on the gloves, skipped around the garage and half-heartedly slugged away at the punchbag.

Without Gran's cheer and civility, Gala's parents found more and more to bicker and wrangle and snap about. Her mother had never been one to bite her tongue for the sake of keeping the peace but when it came to the stamina required for late-night harangues, her father had the upper hand: he could, and did, go on for hours.

What he went on about frequently fell into the *not in front of the children* category but by then the children were adolescents and though sent off to their bedrooms – adjacent, upstairs, away from their parents who slept on the ground floor – they were often far from asleep.

The central heating vents carried sound as well as heat, so Gala and Jas could communicate from one room to the other as easily as if the house had an internal phone system. They could also – and the two of them had long kept this a secret – tune in to the depressing drama of their parents' wrangling. What began as a low simmer would build to a hard boil of oaths and insults. The house hissed, a pressure cooker ready to blow its top.

One night, Miles even brought up the *inconvenience* of Gran dying when she did. If there hadn't been all the arrangements to take care of, and if, into the bargain, he hadn't had to knock his pan in teaching, he could have undoubtedly produced so much more work, so much better work, work which would have got him noticed, made his name, his reputation, secured him a place in posterity. It wasn't Gran's *fault*, of course he wasn't saying that, what did Vera take him for, an utter idiot? – he was just pointing out that, from his point of view, the timing couldn't have been worse.

Bastard, Jas mouthed into the heating vent, then struck a match.

You're too young to smoke, Gala mouthed back.

So are you.

I'm nearly legal, said Gala, lighting up.

What'll you do when you *are* legal?

Get the hell out of here, said Gala.

What about me? What'll I do if you leave home?

I don't know, said Gala. I don't know.

Milestones from different stages of childhood were scattered around her room: a bedraggled teddy bear, a favourite one-armed doll, a pair of threadbare ballet shoes, ice skates she'd long outgrown, a tennis racket she hadn't picked up in years. One day this would no longer be her room. One day she would be out of here and living in a flat with friends her own age. She'd eat curry that wasn't reconstituted from a packet and spaghetti that hadn't been chopped up to fit in a tin can, read Russian poetry and never again have to listen to the bloody marital strife boiling up from the floor below.

Our Lady of the Iguanas

ON A POSTCARD of a woman in a flowery dress, eyes heavenward, half a dozen iguanas clinging to her head:

> *Dear Mum and Dad,*
>   *In Mexico at last! It's November and I'm on the beach. Rented a cabana on a peninsula well off the beaten track. It's pretty basic and I share it with the local pigs, mice and mosquitoes. And an iguana. Amazing things, total throwback to prehistory. Been doing some drawing and painting but the atmosphere's so humid the paints are going mouldy!*
>   *Gala xx*

She didn't mention the rats the size of cats, or the snakes as thick as her arm and twice as long. The peninsula was picturesque but only habitable close to the coast. The land rose steeply, the vegetation was thick and rumour had it that it was dangerous for gringos to venture up the hill. The jungle chorus kept her awake at night. She had no desire to stray far from the coast, from the ferry boat which came once a day and deposited a new load of travellers.

She didn't mention that the main activity amongst the gringos, apart from lying on the beach, sipping on a Corona or a Dos

Equis, thumbing through a Carlos Castaneda title then cooling off in the tepid ocean, trying a spot of fishing or stringing bead bracelets, was getting off their skulls on the local weed. People passed weeks, months, possibly years, in this out-of-the-way, sun-kissed spot, doing little else.

She didn't mention the single male travellers who kept insomnia and the rodent night life at bay. There were a few. She isn't counting. Only one is worth mentioning: tall, blond, soft-spoken, a musical lilt to his voice. Was he German, Swiss, Austrian? He was on a mission. He wasn't just drifting around the continent like the rest of them, waiting to see where he washed up. He was searching for a tribe who lived way up the hill and took a lot of mescal for spiritual enlightenment.

For one blissful night he shared her bed, her body and her mosquito net, then he was off. He travelled light. Everything he needed, he carried in a daypack: notes, a first-aid kit, a change of clothes, a hunting knife. He was fearless but not foolhardy. Perhaps if he'd stuck around she'd have tired of his wisdom beyond his years, his esoteric obsessions. But he didn't and so all that remains is simple, and good.

Still Life with Dimple

THERE WAS ALWAYS the whisky. More of the whisky. Scotch. A bottle in the china cabinet, another somewhere convenient but not too obvious on the studio shelves. How much of the stuff her father got through in a day, or evening – or when he started in on it – was difficult to gauge but he'd pour himself a stiff one the moment he got home from teaching and, throughout the evening, continued to top up his glass.

He didn't drink whisky at mealtimes. Water or milk like the rest of the family. Whisky didn't go with food. At least not her mother's food. Or her mother's abstinence. Vera's *teetotalitarianism,* which he liked to bring up when he was in a nasty mood, which was becoming more often than not. Even if the nastiness didn't come to a head, it was there, always there, pulsing away at his temples. Mealtimes were fraught.

His social drinking was done at the golf club or at the bathing club he'd recently joined which, in addition to a swimming pool, offered Turkish baths, and a bar. A very reasonably priced bar. The pool had monkey rings and trapezes. Every so often, the club hosted a family night and once in a while Gala and Jas were permitted to try out the rings and trapezes. And fantasise about running away to join the circus. But opportunities to swing through space were too few and far between to master the equipment. Even on family nights the grownups – fathers mostly – were far from welcoming: they didn't pay membership fees for other people's brats to get in the way of their sixty lengths, or hog the monkey rings when they wanted to show off their own gymnastic expertise.

When he went on his own, Miles would have his swim, and sometimes a Turkish, before passing some time at the bar. He saw no reason why exercise shouldn't be followed by one or two refreshments. Or three or four. The revised drink-driving laws were still very recent and according to him, nobody felt the need to take them seriously. Nobody, at least, who considered himself a cut above the common man – who of course had to be put and kept firmly in his place – felt the laws actually applied to him. As for the breathalyser, well it didn't stand up in a court of law, did it? His sort – and more to the point, the sort to whose ranks he aspired, considered themselves a law unto themselves. Always had. And acted accordingly. Irresponsibly. When apprehended for speeding offences, their reaction was bluster and bafflement. They were only keeping their end up, weren't they? Living life to the full. If the car you drove was designed to top a hundred and twenty miles per hour, what could be wrong with doing the ton on the open road?

Evening drinking, social or not, was one thing but there was also the daytime drinking. Clandestine. At work. By now, more often than not, Miles was driving his son and daughter home from their respective city schools after a liquid lunch. Vera was aware of his drinking, that much was clear from the snips and mutters about the smell on his breath or his unusual cheeriness but, though she disapproved on principle, it was the potential shame of discovery that bothered her most. And its possible repercussions. Tippling from the Dimple bottle stashed in the art room store cupboard was one thing. Being found out was another.

Passed Over

PASSED OVER! HE snapped. Passed over for promotion in favour of a young, talentless sucker-up, a yes-man who chooses to be on first names terms with his pupils! One of those free-thinking types pressing for educational reform, railing against the war in Vietnam, bandying about names like Martin Luther King and Nelson Mandela, siding with nitwits who sit down in front of tanks! *Make Love, Not War* – who ever heard of such rot! The old order is crumbling, the country going to pot. No respect for elders and betters, that's the problem. For authority. But I, for one, have no intention of trying to bridge the generation gap or the class divide, or of letting standards slip. I intend to let my pupils know who's boss. Start as you mean to go on, that's my motto. Let the blighters know what's in store for them if they step out of line. Make them aware that, where I am concerned, art is not a soft option.

In the dinette, Gala was trying to extract sense from Hamlet's shilly-shallying about life and death. Across the table, Jas was tussling with a maths problem about shifting goods and passengers from one side of a river to the other. Vera was in the kitchen, knocking around some pots. Her approach to housework involved a deal more slamming and banging than Gran's ever had. Miles helped himself to a large whisky, lit a cigarette and dropped his bomb.

The exact words with which he described his actions have been pushed to the back of some deep cerebral recess where they remain. Irretrievable. Indelible. As an introduction to starting as he meant to go on, to letting a new class know who was boss, Gala's father had called all the boys to his desk. They were in their first year of secondary school, new and green and brimming with rumours of bullying and vicious initiation rites; boys whose voices had yet to break; quaking in heavy leather shoes; sweating under starched shirt collars and itchy blazers.

One by one he instructed them to hold out their hands. And one by one belted the entire class, who had, as yet, done nothing right or wrong. One by one their hands had burned from the teacher's trusty aide: the belt, the strap, the trusty tawse, the fork-tongued Lochgelly, speciality of the eponymous town in Fife whose main claim to fame was a length of reinforced leather, designed to cause pain to children.

Prevention is better than cure, he said.

His words dropped into a well of silence.

There's too much *laxity* these days, too much *laissez-faire*. I simply gave them a taste of what they can expect should they not meet my standards of discipline. Let them know I'm a force to be reckoned with. An *authority*. They won't be doing as they please in my class. Oh no, they'll be dancing to my tune.

Season of the Heart

THEN ALONG CAME the next big thing. The heart attack. A big one. Massive, Vera was informed by telephone, a massive heart attack. Nobody, it seemed, would be dancing to Miles's tune for some considerable time.

Gala, Jas and Vera moved through the long hospital corridors without speaking, following the signs to Intensive Care, inhaling without comment the sharp tang of Dettol and carbolic soap, and the complex undertow of illness. Trolley wheels squeaked on the lino. Voices bounced off the walls. Bright chit-chat, laughter. Gala felt detached from her body, distant from it, had lost connection with her own footsteps, heartbeat. The words *heart* and *attack* shuffled around in her head, defied comprehension.

Her mother, breathing fast and shallow, hurrying without appearing to, led the way through a long ward filled with men in pyjamas, propped up on pillows. Asleep or awake, they gaped like stunned, stubbled fish.

There he is! Her mother waved with extravagant cheer, as if they were about to join a party. There's Dad! We came as soon as we could, Miles. I had to collect the children from school and then I got a bit lost rejoining the Great Western Road and then we hit the rush hour traffic.

Miles raised an arm a few inches then let it fall. Jas stood stiffly at the head of the bed. He looked taller, more grown up. At his new school, contact sports were obligatory and he had bulked out. But his lip quivered. He blinked. Gala hung back, suddenly afraid. Her mother tugged at her arm.

Give your father a hug.

He was changed. His skin was a different colour, a greyish pink, like meat gone bad. His pyjama jacket gaped and his chest looked caved-in. He had purple and yellow bruises on his hands. Her mother said not to worry about the bruises, that was where they'd put the drips in, but how did she know so much about everything when they'd only just arrived? The biggest change was in her father's eyes: they were no longer feverishly bright with plans and schemes, or ablaze with irritation; they were dark, wary, fearful.

Did you hear me? said her mother sharply. Give Dad a hug.

Gala didn't even want to look at him in this changed state, didn't know what to do with the information: being told by her mother what to do made the act of greeting all the more awkward than it already was. Her father was lying on his back, tubes attached to his arms and wires to his chest. How was she supposed to hug him without disturbing the drips and monitors? And there were so many people in the ward, all surreptitiously clocking each other: visitors, patients, nurses, all with one eye on how everybody else was behaving, bearing up. All this personal stuff acted out under the harsh ward lights and the scrutiny of strangers.

Her mother bent to kiss him on the cheek. He averted his face. She sat on the only chair and took his hand. He fiddled with his drip. She asked about the food and the nurses, whether it was noisy in the ward, whether he was getting enough sleep. He replied flatly that the food was no worse than army rations. His eyelids flickered and his gaze slid to the ceiling where a fan turned slowly.

Anyway, said Vera. We're here now. That's the main thing.

Yes, said Miles, without a grain of enthusiasm. You're here now.

And what about the nurses?

All sorts, he said. Look around you. Liquorice allsorts.
Miles!

A smiling West Indian nurse was wheeling a medicine
trolley through the ward, waving to visitors and patients alike,
humming and swaying her hips with the easy grace of a boat
bobbing on a warm sea.

At least she didn't hear you, said her mother. You don't want
to get on the wrong side of the nurses, wherever they're from.
Are they looking after you properly?

They do their job.

Well, that's what they're paid for.

She began to fish stuff from her bag: toffees, mints, grapes,
talcum powder, toothpaste. She laid them out on the bedside
table and instructed Jas to fill up the plastic water jug.

I don't know where the sink is.

Oh, just have a nose around, she said breezily, as if all
members of the Price family were perfectly at home in Intensive
Care. Ask a nurse.

He'll be lucky to find one that understands English, said
Miles.

But the nurses are busy, said Jas, flushing, holding up the jug
but staying put.

For heaven's sake, said Vera, do as you're told for once.

I don't need fresh water, said Miles. I didn't ask for water.

But you must drink, or you'll become dehydrated. It's hot in
here. Don't you find it hot? Isn't it too hot to sleep? I couldn't
sleep in this heat.

You don't have to, he said. Think yourself lucky.

I'll get water, said Gala, taking the jug from Jas.

I've already said, I don't bloody need any water!

Don't excite yourself, dear, said Vera. You mustn't excite
yourself. The doctor said –

What I need is a smoke. Did you bring any fags?

I didn't think you'd be allowed to smoke.

Well, you thought wrong. There's a smoking room at the end
of the next corridor. And it's always packed out. So there you are.

Rumpus

WHEN HE WAS discharged from hospital and told to take it easy – something Gala's father found exasperating beyond words – there were other changes. Little things. At first. A clothes brush, for example. He took offence at the clothes brush which Vera had given him. Not at being given one: the smoking habit which he'd resumed at full throttle as soon as he got out, and the studio dust which clung to his clothes and skin, made a clothes brush practical enough.

It was the colour he objected to. Yellow. Not a particularly appealing shade. Not a yolky gamboge or creamy Naples yellow. Cold, acidic: chrome yellow or possibly lemon. Not that he was at all bothered by the specific shade.

Are you saying I'm a coward, is that what you're saying? Are you saying I'm yellow?

Unusually, her mother didn't seem to have an answer. Or else she was quick-witted enough to realise that no answer would do, that any response at all would only add fuel to the flames which were already crackling and snapping.

Is that what you're saying? Well let me tell you, you've got it wrong. Very wrong.

He stormed off, got into the car and gunned up the driveway. Brush in hand, her mother stood at the window. The car lurched onto the street, taking some of the overgrown hedge with it.

Here, Vera said to Gala. You have it. Somebody should use the damn thing. There's nothing wrong with it. All the fuss he's making about the colour is a piece of nonsense.

Gala didn't much like the colour either and didn't want a clothes brush, especially now that it had become a loud reminder of her father's weirdness. But she took it and shoved it in a drawer, alongside the remains of the sari she'd ruined by trying to sew a dress without knowhow or pattern.

Then things seemed to start to go missing, piddly things: nails, a screwdriver, a chisel. Her father had so many nails, screwdrivers and chisels it was a mystery how he noticed any of his tools or implements were missing. But things going missing wasn't the problem, it was the fuss he made about their disappearance. He insisted that he hadn't simply mislaid them, that his wife hadn't simply put them away in the wrong drawer, no, his *wife* – as he began to refer to Vera exclusively – had deliberately hidden them, that her reasons for doing so were to irritate him, to sabotage his work, to make his life a misery. For days he harried her about the whereabouts of a red-handled screwdriver.

Have you seen my screwdriver? I'll ask you again: Have you seen my screwdriver? I'll say it in plain English that any imbecile can understand: What have you done with my screwdriver?

What would I want with a screwdriver? her mother wailed. What good would it be to me?

I didn't say you *wanted* it. I didn't say you had any use for it, did I? Did I?

A harsh light flashed in his eyes. He bared his teeth, clenched his fists. On and on it would go and her mother didn't do what might have been sensible: she didn't humour him, didn't say, *Yes dear, you're quite right, how stupid of me.* It wasn't in Vera's nature to let herself become a pitiful, downtrodden doormat. She stood her ground. Tried to make her husband see sense. Told him he was imagining things. He'd been drinking too much and the booze was polluting his brain. He should lay off the Dimple and calm down, at all costs he should calm down and think about his health. Did he want another heart attack? Did he want to end up in hospital again?

What kind of nitwit do you take me for? he replied.

Miles, you shouldn't excite yourself.

No, you're right about that. I shouldn't excite myself. *You* should excite me. *You* should be more *erotic* and less *neurotic*. That's what *you* should do.

Her mother let that particular barb go. Miles mustn't excite himself. He mustn't be excited. He must be kept calm, mollified. Anything potentially irritating or likely to raise his blood pressure should be kept from him. At first it seemed as though he might just have too much time on his hands, or that the medication he was taking was making him feel unusually out of sorts.

When he could go on the rampage over the colour of a hairbrush or a few missing nails – he accused Vera of giving his nails to a plumber who came to fix the toilet, and of passing on his red-handled screwdriver to Mr Woolf, the piano tuner, adding some snide comments about his wife's interest in a man who had the time and inclination to read the Sunday papers from cover to cover – it wasn't easy to plan ahead, anticipate and thereby insulate him, or anybody else, against upset. Besides, he seemed to want to get worked up, to make a fuss, to cause a stushie. He wanted people to sit up and take note, somehow, any old how; the whole problem was that the world hadn't ever taken enough note of him.

He fell out of love with Marlene. She may have been beautiful, she may have sung like a husky, hell-bent siren but when all was said and done she was, in his opinion, disloyal, a deserter. She had turned her back on her own people. Whatever anybody thought of Hitler, the fact was that Germany was her homeland, her nation. And to her compatriots, she was a traitor. And traitors should get what they deserved. He stopped playing Marlene's records. He left them lying about the studio, cast loose from their protective sleeves, gathering dust, scratches, rings from coffee cups and whisky glasses.

Loyalty – the lack of it – desertion and betrayal became his favourite obsessions. His parents had let him down, his brother and sister had feathered their own nests, the people he should have been able to depend on when the chips were down had short-changed him, left him in the lurch. His wife couldn't be trusted, his children didn't respect his authority.

One morning, after raking through his filing cabinet, he pulled out his army discharge papers and thrust them in Vera's face.

See, *I* was a soldier. *I* was not a coward. *I* was not a deserter. *I* was not a traitor. *I* was loyal. Honourable discharge. Read it. *Read it!*

There was nothing much Vera could say to this but no response was as suspect as the wrong response. He gunned up the driveway once more. This time he made multiple copies of his discharge papers – negotiating a cheap rate for a hundred – and announced his intention to repaper the tangerine walls of the living room with Xeroxes of his honourable discharge. Lest anybody forget.

Vera must have somehow got the message across to him that as a repeating pattern, his discharge papers weren't very appealing – or artistic – as he didn't get around to carrying out his threat of covering the walls with them. He framed the original and hung it next to the group photo of his army outfit. Ex-service bridge partners continued to be sought via the small ads but failed to materialise.

Some long nights of heated harangue proved too much for Vera. In the small hours, she fled down the road, on occasion in nightie, dressing gown and slippers, and chapped the door of the manse. Reverend Balquidder's wife provided tea, sympathy, blankets and a couch on which to spend the remainder of the night. In the morning she returned home, tense and snivelly.

As Miles continued to find fault with the world in general and his wife and children in particular, Gala became gloomy and morbid. At school she avoided the feeding frenzy in the cafeteria, its perennial pong of tuna fish and egg mayonnaise and the chastening sight of fat girls eating themselves fatter, preferring to spend her lunch hour alone at the top of the school, gazing down into the stairwell.

Jas grew taller and stronger than Gala. He plunged into

thrashing rock music and began to grow his hair. Schools were beginning to relax their rules, to come round to the idea that a short back and sides needn't always be synonymous with academic excellence or moral backbone. By then, people knew a bit more about what had really gone on in Vietnam.

Vera, with some pointless loyalty to conformity, felt the need to nag Jas about the length of his hair. It would upset Dad, she insisted. And, as she was to repeat like a five-finger exercise, Dad must not, for any reason, be upset. Fixated as he was with the suspect colour of a clothes brush, the whereabouts of screwdrivers, the betrayal of Marlene Dietrich, Miles didn't pay a blind bit of notice to the length of his son's hair. Until Vera took it upon herself to alert him to it.

When he did notice, he became fixated with that as well. Long hair on men denoted lack of backbone, subversive tendencies, laziness, dubious masculinity. Long hair was symptomatic of every social ill of the moment. As Jas, rebelliously, repeatedly refused to get a haircut, Miles waited until he was asleep – the kid slept soundly in those days – crept into his bedroom, and gave him the worst crew cut this side of the Atlantic. Overnight, Jas became surly and closed off. Whenever both parents were simultaneously out of the house – more often separately than together – he cranked up the volume of Led Zeppelin, Black Sabbath, The Who, and beat the shit out of his punchbag.

In the winter of that year Gala's father once more began to cultivate his whiskers, Victorian-style, and to snarl at himself in the mirror. And to heat things up a bit, to keep everyone on their toes, especially his wife, whose name he seemed to have forgotten or become disinclined to pronounce, he brought home a shotgun.

The Pips

IT MIGHT HAVE been the sound of the pipes drifting down from the slopes of Popocatépetl which brought on a snivel of homesickness, or cash running out, travel fatigue setting in. Or, simply, it was time. To revisit; review.

Apart from her parents, nobody was keenly awaiting Gala's return. No loose ends in her love life, no significant other to get back to, for. Friends were getting on with their lives. Before she left, her contemporaries were already getting hitched and settling into proper jobs with paid holidays, power dressing, in-jokes, prospects. They'd buckled down, put their shoulders to the wheel, their noses to the grindstone, as Gala's mother had reminded her, in the hope that her wayward daughter would follow suit. Gala didn't envy her friends their spouses, status or salaries but their certainty, the smug glow which came from believing you'd made the right move, taken the correct turn – *that* she hankered for. Her own path rambled, hit dead ends.

She wrote home, occasionally; phoned rarely. Long distance calls were costly and a hassle: faulty phoneboxes, incompatible time zones, bad reception, desperadoes on the streets making obscene gestures on other side of the glass.

Hi, it's me.

Oh hello, hello, where are you?

Still in Mexico. How's everybody?

Oh fine, fine. Well, Dad's not been great. Did you get my last letter?

Not sure. What was it about?

It doesn't matter now. Dad's okay, now, he's okay. And your brother, well you know about that.

Yes, it's a shame.

I never trusted that wife of his, not from the word go –

How are *you*?

Oh, fine, I suppose. You'll have to come and see the new house when you get back – when *are* you likely to get back?

Not sure yet. Keep you posted.

Shall I get your father? He'd like to say hello. I'm sure he'd like to say hello.

If he's not down at the end of the garden. This phonebox is gulping down the coins.

I'll tell him to be quick – Miles, Miles, it's Gala, *Gala*, your *daughter*, on the phone, calling long distance! Somewhere in Mexico. I didn't catch the name of the place. You'll have to be quick, Miles, or she'll be cut off... He's coming. Here he is, here's Dad.

Hi Dad.

Hello Gala.

How are you, Dad?

Fine. How are you, Gala?

I'm fine. What have you been up to?

Not a lot.

How's the new house?

Fine. It's fine. Big garden, a lot to do in the garden. I'm thinking of planting asparagus. Well, your mother wants another word so... cheerio.

Bye Dad.

Hello dear. Thanks for your postcard, by the way. I'm building up quite a collection. And adding to my stamp album! The American stamps are a bit dull but the Mexican ones are very pretty. I know Dad doesn't say much but he's pleased to hear your voice, he really is. I'll tell your brother you called. He's in a caravan right now. All he can afford due to that bitch –

Mum, that's my last coin –
The things she's put him through. And Dad's been, he's not
been –
Mum, that's the pips –

A Whispering Gallery

THERE WAS A whispering gallery. In the house, on the street, at school, in the studio, everywhere an echo chamber of slights and putdowns. They were out to get him. *What are you talking about Miles? Who's out to get you?* Who do she think? Women. For a start. Women who were disloyal to their husbands. Why was it his wife knew so many divorcees and spinsters, why was she drawn to women who couldn't cope with men or preferred not to, to women men didn't want or care for, women whose marriages had failed, or had never got off the ground in the first place, why was that exactly? What's the answer, what's the answer?

Why didn't his wife associate with normal women, normal married women, with good wives, patient, supportive, obliging, easygoing, well turned out, *loyal* wives, wives who were erotic rather than neurotic, wives who did what their husbands wanted, in or out of bed, wives who didn't let themselves go, who didn't nag, sag, wives who didn't bunk off in the middle of the night, preferring the minister's lumpy couch to the warmth of the marital bed? Why did his wife have to become one of them?

And when he went back to teaching, when the sick pay ran out and he was officially designated fit to work once more, when he had to go back and face the bloody staffroom backstabbers and those in promoted posts who looked down their superior superannuated noses at him, as if he were little better than a minion, they were out to get him too: to do him down; pass him over; see him get his comeuppance; watch him fail and fall in the fiery furnace.

And did they just stand by idly waiting for it to happen? Oh no, they gave him a hearty, helping hand, sped him on his way, pushed him towards the edge. They didn't just wash their hands of the whole thing, no no, don't you believe it. They were pushing, prodding, nudging, shoving; they wanted to see him fall, drop, sink, burning as he fell. That was what would give them pleasure, that was what their pleasure amounted to, that was all he'd got for his efforts: betrayal.

His eyes burned, his head burned. It was hot in his head, so hot, so full of noise, such a furnace, chock-a-block with the blare of burning, the hot roar of flame-throwers, the crackle and spit, the hiss and sizzle, it was hot hot hot in his head and busy, it was crowded, packed to the gills with whispers, crackling whispers, his skull was roasting, sizzling, his skull was spitting and splitting on a hot skillet, his brain was burning up.

Whisky and cigarettes fanned the flames and sleep wouldn't come. Not at all. The eyes could not be shut, they were too hot to shut, the lids would melt, the lids would fuse together, the whispering would get trapped inside fused eyelids and then what, then what? The eyes must be kept open at all times, he must keep watch because they were out to get him and if he dropped his guard, they'd see their chance, and move right in. *Who is out to get you, Miles? Who would move in? What would they move into?*

Couldn't stop, couldn't stay still, staying still made you a sitting duck, an easy target, keep on the move, on your toes, trust no-one, not even your nearest and dearest, especially your nearest, your nearest are not your dearest, no, no, don't let them fool you, your dearest are long gone, your dearest are far, far away, nobody remembers who they are, their names have been erased, eaten up, burnt out. Give them an inch and they'll take a liberty, a page out of your book, a day out of your life. Vigilance at all times.

And under the bed, a loaded gun, which of course, if you have in your possession, you are at some point going to use. Stands to reason, doesn't it? A gun you bring out and clean, in full view of your wife and teenage children, a gun you remove it from its canvas casing, hold it up so they can see it, every one of them, every one of these people who call themselves your family, hold it up to let them know you mean business. You don't buy a gun to amuse yourself, you buy a gun to keep your family on their toes and anybody else, for that matter, who wants to do you down –

You test the moving parts, make sure everything is in working order. Got to be ready, on the alert, on red alert, got to be prepared for anything any one of them might throw at you, vigilance at all times, vigilance is all, there were out to get him but he'd put up a fight, he'd damn well put up the fight of his life, he'd show them he was made of tougher stuff than they thought, he wasn't some limp-wristed nancy boy, some crawling yellow-bellied turncoat, he'd show them, he'd show them all – *Who, Miles, who?*

You know who I'm talking about, what I'm talking about, you're in on it, you're all in on it, you're on their side, that's the problem, you should be loyal to me, but you're not, you've deserted me and you know what happens to deserters, don't you? Deserters are lined up against the wall. You're not on my side so you must be on theirs – *Whose side, Miles, whose side?*

It was hospital again for Gala's father, but this time it wasn't his pumping red heart the doctors had to attend to but the grey matter, the burning ring of grey matter inside his head through which he could not stop falling.

And now, after putting a continent between herself and her family, Gala is at the door of The Pleasance, her mother gripping her wrist more tightly than is comfortable, the smell of toasting oatmeal in the air. The door has large panels of reinforced glass. Inside, the hallway is bright and opens out into a spacious dayroom where two dishevelled men, in pyjamas and slippers, are playing pool. One wears a leather crash helmet and intermittently dunts his head against the table. The other is her father.

The door is locked to keep the patients safe, says her mother. Ring the bell. You have to ring the bell if you want to go in.

Selected Stories
Dilys Rose
ISBN: 978 1 842820773 PBK £7.99

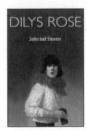

A compelling compilation by the award-winning Scottish writer Dilys Rose, selected from her previous books.

In stories told from a wide range of perspectives and set in many parts of the world, Rose examines everyday lives on the edge through an unforgettable cast of characters.

With subtlety, wit and dark humour, she demonstrates her seemingly effortless command of the short story form at every twist and turn of these deftly poised and finely crafted stories.

Lord of Illusions
Dilys Rose
ISBN: 978 1 842820776 PBK £7.99

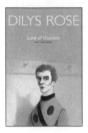

Exploring the human condition in all its glory – and all its folly – *Lord of Illusions* treats both with humour and compassion.

Often wry, always thought-provoking, this new collection offers intriguing glimpses into the minds and desires of a diverse cast of characters; from jockey to masseuse, from pornographer to magician, from hesitant transvestite to far- from-home aid worker.

Each of these finely crafted stories, with their subtle twists and turns, their changes of mood and tone, demonstrate the versatile appeal of the short story, for which Dilys Rose is deservedly celebrated.

Bodywork

Dilys Rose

ISBN: 1905222939 PBK £8.99

How do we feel about the flesh that surrounds us and how do we deal with the knowledge that it will eventually do so no more? How do our bodies affect our emotional, physical and spiritual lives?

Body Work focuses on the human body in all its glory, comedy and frailty; on the quirks, hazards and conundrums of physiology; on intimations of mortality – and immortality. Rose draws fully-grown characters in a few vivid strokes; from a body double to a cannibal queen, their souls are personified in a limb, affliction or skill. These poems get under your skin and into your bones – you'll never look at the human body in the same way again!

Dilys Rose exposes and illuminates humanity with scalpel sharpness... ingeniously exciting, quirky and perceptive.
JANET PAISLEY, THE SCOTSMAN

Brave and unusual, full of unexpected insights and delights...
CATHERINE SMITH

Da Happie Laand

Robert Alan Jamieson

ISBN 9781906817862 PBK £9.99

In the summer of the year of the Millennium, a barefoot stranger comes to the door of the manse for help. But three days later he disappears without trace, leaving a bundle of papers behind.

Da Happie Laand weaves the old minister's attempt to make sense of the mysteries left behind by his 'lost sheep' – the strange tale of a search for his missing father at midsummer – with an older story relating the fate of a Zetlandic community across the centuries, the tales of those people who emigrated to New Zetland in the South Pacific, and those who stayed behind.

Jamieson's strange masterpiece Da Happie Laand haunts dreams and waking hours, as it takes my adopted home of Shetland, twisting it and the archipelago's history into the most disturbing, amazing, slyly funny shapes.
TOM MORTON, SUNDAY HERALD

Luath Press Limited

committed to publishing well written books worth reading

LUATH PRESS takes its name from Robert Burns, whose little collie Luath (*Gael.*, swift or nimble) tripped up Jean Armour at a wedding and gave him the chance to speak to the woman who was to be his wife and the abiding love of his life. Burns called one of the 'Twa Dogs' Luath after Cuchullin's hunting dog in Ossian's *Fingal*. Luath Press was established in 1981 in the heart of Burns country, and is now based a few steps up the road from Burns' first lodgings on Edinburgh's Royal Mile. Luath offers you distinctive writing with a hint of unexpected pleasures.

Most bookshops in the UK, the US, Canada, Australia, New Zealand and parts of Europe, either carry our books in stock or can order them for you. To order direct from us, please send a £sterling cheque, postal order, international money order or your credit card details (number, address of cardholder and expiry date) to us at the address below. Please add post and packing as follows: UK – £1.00 per delivery address; overseas surface mail – £2.50 per delivery address; overseas airmail – £3.50 for the first book to each delivery address, plus £1.00 for each additional book by airmail to the same address. If your order is a gift, we will happily enclose your card or message at no extra charge.

Luath Press Limited

543/2 Castlehill
The Royal Mile
Edinburgh EH1 2ND
Scotland
Telephone: +44 (0)131 225 4326 (24 hours)
Fax: +44 (0)131 225 4324
email: sales@luath. co.uk
Website: www. luath.co.uk